THE HABITATS O

Luis Feder

THE HABITATS OF ALLCON

Luis Feder

Impressum

Die automatisierte Analyse des Werkes, um daraus Informationen insbesondere über Muster, Trends und Korrelationen gemäß §44b UrhG („Text und Data Mining") zu gewinnen, ist untersagt.

© 2024 Luis Feder

Verlag: BoD · Books on Demand GmbH, In de Tarpen 42, 22848 Norderstedt

Druck: Libri Plureos GmbH, Friedensallee 273, 22763 Hamburg

ISBN: 978-3-7693-1874-6

THE HABITATS OF ALLCON

Luis Feder

Contents:
Chapters:
Foreword
Chapter 1. Day-to-Day Life
Chapter 2. Arrival
Chapter 3. Habitat
Chapter 4. Hope
Chapter 5. Respiration
Chapter 6. Representatives
Chapter 7. Dialogue
Chapter 8. Todax
Chapter 9. Downward Spiral
Chapter 10. Freedom Fighters
Chapter 11. Judgment
Chapter 12. Assistance
Chapter 13. Unexpected
Chapter 14. Proof
Acknowledgments

Foreword

Disclaimer:

All names, characters, and events in this book are fictional and entirely invented. Any resemblance to actual persons, living or dead, or real events is purely coincidental. The author therefore expressly disclaims any potential claims related to these similarities.

Copyright:

This book is protected by copyright. Copying, reprinting, public performance, or distribution in any form, whether in full or in part, is prohibited without the explicit permission of the author and will be prosecuted. Texts, graphics, and illustrations by Luis Feder.

Copyright © 2019

Translated from the German original using artificial intelligence .

Special thanks to the team at OpenAI

Journey Through Life

Through the mind we roam;
Doubt sank below,
Fear let go;
And opened gates to home.

At first, a narrow trail;
Experience taught,
And to a wide path brought,
To keep and never fail!

Whole worlds arise,
Vast and free,
Where deeds and words lose ties,
Beyond all time and humanity.

Now, all makes sense at last;
Pure power reveals its might;
A harvest from the past,
A triumph from the fight.

Where no one's harmed or bled,
Where no fright takes hold;
Only here, as has been said,
Is a judgment good and bold!

Poem by Luis Feder

Copyright © 2019

1. Day-to-Day Life

Berlin, Germany's beautiful capital. It was a warm summer day in the heart of Berlin, and there was something special about the city in summertime. Though modern Berlin still bore the scars of its political past, these wounds were slowly healing. Of course, the last world war wasn't so long ago. There were still people alive who had witnessed it firsthand, although they were becoming fewer each year. The young Nazis of that era were now old men and women, and the survivors who had fled back then now had descendants of their own. Ultimately, Berlin had come to embrace the idea that Earth was a shared home for all nations, with space enough for everyone in abundance.

The architecture was a mix of old and new. Some of the beautiful old buildings had been repurposed into museums, while others had been painstakingly restored after being damaged. And then there were the impressive modern structures—tall, striking, and beautiful. It was a symphony of old and new. Everywhere, life was thriving. Green spaces were lush and flourishing. Bright, fragrant flowers and deep green leaves brightened the cityscape, and birds filled the air with their songs—along with, of course, the buzzing of insects.

Lennart was single. It wasn't that he was unattractive or that he couldn't be charming, but he didn't feel he had much to offer. His relationships fizzled out quickly because he wasn't financially able to go out much, which left his dates feeling he was either a little boring or a bit stingy. Not willing to go out of his way to live beyond his means just to "buy" companionship, he decided to keep to himself. He saw himself as the master of his own fate and believed he could be happy on his own. When he did want to be around people, as he did that day, he'd head to Berlin's city center, where he could be among the crowds. He lived a few kilometers north of Berlin in a small 45-square-meter apartment. Occasionally, he'd meet up with his one true friend, Felix. His parents lived in southern Germany, and he'd sometimes call his mother and pass along his regards to his father. All in all, he was doing well.

Though he was a 33-year-old adult, Lennart had an obvious fear of insects. It was often so childish and unfounded that he'd keep his windows shut on hot evenings just to make sure nothing could crawl or fly in. His friend Felix had once advised him to put insect screens on his windows so he could let in some fresh air at night and avoid suffocating. But because Lennart never took his advice, Felix would tease him a bit, though he kept it lighthearted and never went too far. Once, Felix joked dryly about Lennart's single status and his aversion to insects: "Hey, Lenni, if you happen to meet a 'fly girl' with huge black eyes, don't just run away." After a pause, he'd continued with a serious face, "It's just sunglasses, not compound eyes!" They'd known each other for years and understood each other well.

On this particular day, dressed lightly in jean shorts and a loose cotton T-shirt suited to the warm weather, Lennart was standing in a very crowded post office downtown. In his left hand, he carried a dozen small packages in a large plastic bag. The people in the line grumbled, which was understandable, as no one liked waiting. Most felt it was outright rude that, in such a busy post office, only two of the six service windows were staffed. Behind him, someone in the crowd muttered, "This is ridiculous! The least they could do is put a fan out here if they're going to skimp on staff!"

Lennart wasn't thrilled about it either. The poor air and the heat were starting to get to him, but he'd promised himself not to let anything ruin his good mood. After a few unsuccessful days, he'd finally made some online sales, and he was here to ship his items to his customers. The slow pace was frustrating, but the thought that he could once again cover all his bills with his online business made the wait more bearable.

His business was based on making his own products. He had a 3D printer at home and used it to produce small, everyday items as orders came in, helping him keep afloat. He'd print things like combs, chess sets, phone holders, and he was always coming up with new ideas. This time, he'd managed to sell some plastic car parts to several customers, which was turning out to be pretty profitable.

And so, there he stood, sweating in line, telling himself, "Thank goodness—this month's covered." His goal was to live entirely off his webshop income. Though it was tough sometimes to make ends meet, he'd always found a way to get by. He felt as happy as a kid, knowing he'd be able to cover rent, utilities, car insurance, gas, and internet, and still have enough left for food. And this was just the first week of the month.

Since he had time to kill, he decided to call his buddy, Felix, to share his good mood. "Hey Felix, what's up? I have something to tell you…" The call ended up being pretty long, but that was the point; it helped pass the time. By the time he hung up, there were only three people left ahead of him in line. "Alright, man, I'll catch up with you later." Glancing at his phone (something he did out of habit), he noticed his battery was down to just 12%. But since he only had a quick shopping trip planned, he didn't mind much, even though he'd forgotten his charger at home. Normally, he checked his email regularly to see if any new orders had come in.

Finally, his turn came, and once he'd finished that important task, he got into his car and drove to a big supermarket nearby. He was in a good mood and felt like treating himself because the past few months had been full of financial stress and sacrifices. There were nights he'd woken up from worry and couldn't fall back asleep. Many times, he'd thought about giving up because working so hard for barely enough money just didn't feel worth it. But today, he was optimistic and wanted to reward himself. So, he went up to the cheese counter and asked the clerk if they still had a piece of the delicious French Saint-Nectaire cheese. He loved this cheese. Somewhat indifferently, she replied, "Yes, we have it. How much do you want?" Lennart answered, "Eight slices, please." She quickly cut eight slices, wrapped them up, and put them on the counter without asking if he needed anything else. He took his beloved cheese without a word and put it in his cart. He grumbled inwardly, a bit annoyed by the clerk's lack of friendliness.

Then he wandered through the aisles, adding two bottles of water and a pack of whole-grain bread to his cart. He still felt good. Maybe it was the soothing music playing quietly throughout the store or the following announcement: "Dear customers, become a grill master! At our meat counter, you'll find our summer specials on sausages. Our friendly staff is here to assist you for any occasion." Lennart chuckled a little and thought, "If 'friendly staff' includes the lady at the cheese counter, then that barbecue will surely be a hit." He was looking forward to going home and having a sandwich with his favorite cheese. This cheese was usually too expensive for him to buy regularly, but today was a treat for his taste buds.

He was surprised to realize how carefully he'd had to watch every cent in recent months and how he'd barely managed to get by. He'd even neglected his car the whole time. Sometimes the engine would stutter in third gear, but there was nothing he could do except get used to its quirks. The car was old, a bit rusty here and there, but it got him from point A to point B. He shrugged slightly and went straight to the checkout line. Compared to the post office, this line was quite short. It would have been twice as fast, though, if the guy in front of him hadn't bought so much. He could have let Lennart go ahead with his small purchase, but it was what it was.

Finally, it was Lennart's turn, and he was quickly through the line. He left the store briskly, loaded his groceries into the trunk, and took off with the window open. After all, he still had quite a drive ahead. Lennart lived outside the city, driving from downtown to the northern outskirts. Rent was at least somewhat affordable out there. He drove down the long Kantstraße, which eventually became Neue Kantstraße. Soon, he hit a major roundabout and found himself in a real traffic jam—typical for Berlin at this time of day. He crawled forward for half an hour, barely making any progress. Eventually, Kantstraße became Heerstraße, which stretched out even further. He knew the cheese needed to stay cool in this warm weather. Soon, he'd reach Staaken and leave Berlin. By then, the traffic should've cleared up. But it didn't. He looked far ahead between the cars and saw nothing but traffic stretching as far as he could see. He kept checking his phone for the time; it was already showing a low battery of eight percent at the supermarket.

There were just too many cars on the road. Finally, he saw a left turn onto a small forest road toward Kladow. It was a detour of a few kilometers, but he knew this small, narrow, and secluded road was rarely busy, and he could smoothly drive home that way. A real insider's tip. Once he turned, he breathed a sigh of relief—this little trick had left the traffic jam behind him. He drove along the forest road for quite a while.

It was still quite a distance to his home. The endless wait at the post office, then the grocery shopping, and the long traffic jam made the day pass by in what felt like a blur.

The battery had died, and the phone turned off with a pleasant melody. "Oh well," he thought to himself; he'd be home soon enough and could charge it there. It was early evening by now, and he was getting really hungry. But more than that, he was thirsty. The whole ordeal had really worn him out. Dusk had begun to settle quietly around him. He debated stopping briefly to grab the water from the trunk since he still had about 18 kilometers to go. "Might as well," he said to himself and pulled over to the side of the forest road. He turned off the engine but left the key in the ignition. When he opened the driver's door, he noticed that there wasn't a soul in sight.

He slowly got out and retrieved the shopping bag from the trunk, with the wonderful cheese, whole-grain bread, and water inside. Then he got back into the car and spread everything out on the passenger seat. At this time, no other cars were passing through this part of the forest. Technically, he could have kept driving and would've been home soon, but his thirst got the better of him. Eagerly, he opened the bottle and drank with big, loud gulps. Pausing for a breath, he noticed a swarm of mosquitoes in the air. Lennart hated mosquitoes. He quickly rolled the window up; there must have been a pond or lake or some other water source nearby.

Yes — Lennart and insects. But the ones that bit or sucked blood were especially off-putting to him. He capped the water bottle and set it on the seat next to him. "Mmm, Saint-Nectaire," he whispered softly. He couldn't resist and opened up both the cheese and the bread. Then he placed two slices of cheese perfectly onto the bread, covering it entirely. What a treat. He forgot everything else around him and took his time savoring his sandwich. After finishing the first one, he promptly made another, assembling it with the same precision. He enjoyed the second sandwich just as much.

Outside, it was gradually growing darker. Lennart packed everything back into the bag and placed it behind the passenger seat, but it kept tipping over. He picked up the bag, quickly got out of the car, and in record time, tossed it back into the trunk to keep the flying insects from biting him. The air outside had turned refreshingly cool. He got back in the car, buckled his seatbelt, and turned the key to start the engine. "Chug... chug... chug... chug." The car wouldn't start. "Huh, what's this?" he said out loud. Nervously, he tried five more times in quick succession, but nothing happened. "This can't be happening," he thought, panic setting in. "Damn it!" he muttered to himself. What was he supposed to do? He had to think of every possible way to get help here in the middle of the woods.

He instinctively reached into his right front pocket and pulled out the dead phone. He turned it on, hoping for just enough battery to call his friend Felix to come to the rescue. The phone turned on, and just as he entered his unlock PIN, it went off again with that familiar, soothing melody. He tried again, but this time, it wouldn't turn on at all. It was completely drained. "Oh no!" he groaned in frustration. If only he'd remembered the charging cable. Right now, that cable would've been the easiest solution to his problem. From here on out, he would need to keep a clear head. He had to make a decision.

He mentally went over his options: wait for a car to pass by and hope for a jump start, walk back to the main road where he'd been stuck in traffic, walk straight home, try to fix the car somehow by himself, or spend the night in the car and look for help in the morning. As the darkness set in, he understood he'd need to find a solution fast.

He immediately dismissed the idea of sleeping in the car. Spending the whole night alone in the woods felt creepy. Walking all the way back to the main road to try and find a phone? If he used that same effort to walk toward his apartment, he'd be home before long, and he could deal with the car the next day in peace. He chose that option. First, he'd try to get the car started. If that didn't work, he'd make his way home directly. And if he came across anyone or a passing car along the way, he'd ask for help. That seemed like the most logical approach.

With that, he pulled the stiff lever under the steering wheel to unlock the hood. He switched on the headlights, jumped out, and went around to stand in front of the hood. Reaching under the grille, he released the small safety latch and opened the hood. Under the dim light, he checked the battery connections, jiggling every wire and cable he could find. He couldn't see much, but even if he'd had better light, it wouldn't have helped much, since he didn't really know much about cars. He lowered the hood and latched it shut, got back in the car, and turned the key in the ignition again. Nothing happened. The car still wouldn't start.

Quickly, he got out again, went to the trunk, and took out the warning triangle. He unfolded it and set it visibly on the rear shelf. Then he took out the bag with the groceries. He pulled out the keys, locked all the doors, paused briefly, and then set off at a brisk pace in the direction he'd been driving. His sense of direction told him to stay on the right. If he spotted any shortcut, he'd take it immediately to save time.

At first, he walked with lots of energy and large strides, scratching his head frequently because he kept feeling like he was getting bitten by mosquitoes. He'd slap his neck, then his thigh. The further he went, the itchier he felt all over. He started to sweat. The footpath branched southeast off the road, which would save him valuable time. But his head was spinning with all sorts of negative thoughts. After about forty-five minutes of walking, it was getting very dark, but his eyes had adjusted to the night well enough. He could still make out the silhouettes of trees and bushes. He decided to stick to the rough path to get home faster. So Lennart, driven by his fear, walked on like clockwork, slipping deeper into the forest without noticing. His legs and arms were already covered in mosquito bites, and he even felt bites on his forehead, just above his left eyebrow. He'd scratched that spot so much and so hard that he eventually realized he'd scraped the skin. He felt a stinging sensation and some dampness under his fingernails and above his brow. Now he was bleeding, too. He felt more and more at the mercy of nature.

The path grew narrower, blending seamlessly into the denser forest. It was pitch black. The uneven ground looked like a black void. He could only make out the shapes of nearby trees. He felt like he was still walking in the right direction, but after about an hour of walking, he was exhausted. Resting wasn't an option, though. He drank as he walked. The grocery bag felt heavier with every step as his exhaustion increased. Before long, he'd finished one of the two water bottles and tossed it on the ground. It felt good to quench his thirst and lighten the load at the same time. He wanted to be well-provisioned when he finally made it home. He could've eaten the cheese along the way if he'd felt hungry. And so he kept going for the next hour, walking steadily, weaving his way toward the safety of home. Occasionally, he took a sip from the second bottle. The bag kept switching hands. He was gradually ignoring the increasingly frequent mosquito bites on his arms and legs.

He was sweating more and more, and the exhaustion was becoming impossible to ignore. Clearly, something had gone wrong with his calculations. He'd figured he'd reach the edge of the forest in two hours if he'd gone in the right direction. By now, he should be close to his town. But there was no sign of it. He was worn out and scared to the bone. The forest swallowed the ambient light and all sound. Lennart felt utterly helpless in the face of his own fear. Nervously, he scratched at the countless bites covering his body. He was lost. He no longer knew which way to go. At some point, he'd veered off course. He should have made it through the forest by now.

Overcome by exhaustion, his pace slowed. The slower he went, the colder he felt. He could barely see anything anymore. The ground was uneven, and he jumped at every little noise he made, glancing frantically around himself. Then, he accidentally stepped on a thick, dry branch, and the sharp snap froze him in place. His heart raced. He resolved to get out of this dark forest as quickly as possible, no matter what it took.

In his hurry, not watching the uneven ground, he stumbled, his left foot catching on a solid tree root. He tried instinctively to regain his balance, lunging forward, but couldn't get his right foot in place quickly enough and tumbled forward uncontrollably. His bag of groceries fell from his hand as he crashed to the ground, arms outstretched to break his fall. "Ouch!" he yelled out. Lennart lay flat on his stomach, every muscle in his body tensed. At least he had managed to shield his face from the uneven ground with his outstretched hands. Shocked from the fall, he lay there motionless for a few seconds, breathing in the intense, earthy scent of the forest floor, close to his nose. He could practically taste the ground. His T-shirt had ridden up, exposing the cold leaves beneath his skin. He started cursing under his breath, repeating over and over like a mantra, "Damn it, damn it, damn it!"

He quickly tried to get up, pushing himself off the ground with his hands. He got to his knees and tried to stand, but his left ankle throbbed, and putting weight on it was agonizing. He brushed the dirt and leaves off his body, noticing his hands and face were smudged with grime. Scrapes on his thighs burned like tiny fires, caused by sharp stones he'd slid over as he fell. His T-shirt was filthy all over, but right now, he couldn't care less. He'd twisted his ankle badly, and all he could do was hobble with a pain-wracked expression, doing his best to keep weight off his left foot. The cool air gave him goosebumps. Slowly, his whispered "damn it" mantra faded as he tried to calm himself. He looked around, hoping to spot a branch or stick he could use as a crutch, but he couldn't see anything. What was he supposed to do now?

Instinctively, he looked for any kind of shape that might serve as a shelter. He knew he wouldn't get far. His apartment, his car, the road — all of it felt impossibly distant. There was only one idea left to him: find some sort of shelter and wait it out until his ankle felt better. Then — he saw something. About 20 meters away, a large, overgrown boulder or piece of rock jutted out of the ground. Picking up the bag he'd dropped nearby, he hobbled determinedly toward the rock formation. His face twisted in pain, fear, and exhaustion as he reached his target. He found a hollow space big enough for him if he curled up. The rock was thickly covered in shrubs and partly blanketed with moss.

At least he'd found a small shelter where he could endure the menacing night with some protection. It dawned on him that he'd made a bad decision. If only he'd stayed in the car—he could have locked the doors from the inside and reclined the padded driver's seat. That would have been like a "five-star hotel" compared to this Stone Age hideout. He clutched the shopping bag to his chest and squeezed into the small crevice, pressing his back against the leafy, branch-covered wall to make a little more room for himself.

Then everything happened in a flash. The overgrown wall that Lennart had mistakenly thought was solid gave way, and he fell backward, tumbling a good two meters into a pitch-black void. With a dull thud, he landed on his back and the back of his head, and at that moment, he lost consciousness.

Meanwhile, Felix was sitting with Nicole and Evelyn at a café in northern Berlin, a popular, trendy spot. They were lounging on one of the many wooden benches on the summer terrace, enjoying the atmosphere. The place was filled with friendly people chatting about everything under the sun, laughing and having animated conversations. In the background, relaxed electronic chillout music played, and bits of conversation and laughter floated in from all directions. The waitstaff bustled about, bringing beautifully arranged salads, drinks, and endless snacks to the tables.

Felix had met Nicole a few weeks back through a coworker who was throwing a small birthday gathering. They'd started talking, hit it off, and exchanged phone numbers. After a few dates, Felix suggested they do a group hangout sometime. Being a bit of a sly one, he asked Nicole to bring along her best friend, so she showed up tonight with Evelyn in tow, and Felix thought it'd be a good opportunity to introduce Evelyn to his single friend, Lennart.

As the three of them relaxed and laughed together, he found himself trying repeatedly to get through to Lennart, but with no luck. Part of him was a little disappointed, and part of him was a bit worried—after all, it wasn't like Lennart to just switch off his phone. "Hmm, that's strange," he commented. "We talked earlier today, and he said he'd check in with me later. This just isn't like him." But, distracted by the company of two charming women, he brushed off the worry. They laughed, cheerfully sipped wine spritzers, and chatted enthusiastically, well into the night.

Whenever the conversation turned back to Lennart, Felix tried calling him again using his phone's speed dial. Eventually, he gave up and left a message on Lennart's voicemail: "Hey, Lenni, it's Felix. Just wanted you to know your buddy here's thinking of you! I'll fill you in when we see each other next. Enjoy your evening—I'm sure doing that here!"

Later, Evelyn began to feel like a bit of a third wheel and apologized, saying she didn't want to intrude on Felix and Nicole. But Felix wasn't having any of it and insisted she stay a bit longer, promising he'd drive both her and Nicole home. He'd kept to the spritzers, after all, to make sure he could still drive. They continued chatting for a little while longer, ordered the check, and each contributed their share as the waitress went around collecting payments.

Together, they piled into Felix's car, and after a 15-minute drive, they reached Evelyn's place. She got out and said goodbye with a parting, "Well, maybe next time your friend Lennart can join us." Felix then dropped Nicole off at her place. Despite the failed attempt to make it a group outing, he hoped she'd enjoyed the evening. He asked her if she'd had a good time, and she smiled, said yes, gave him a quick kiss on the cheek, waved, and disappeared into the hallway of her building. Content and relaxed, Felix drove home.

2. Arrival

In his unconscious state, dreamlike images washed over Lennart. He floated almost weightlessly, free of pain, lying on his back as if on a gentle surface of water, lifted up and down by soft, rhythmic waves. The motion felt like the gentle rocking of a loving mother singing her baby to sleep. He felt so free, so light, completely unburdened. Everything around him was warm and peaceful, calm and familiar.

Suddenly, Lennart's eyes snapped open. He'd come to, realizing with alarm that he couldn't breathe. His lungs must have been bruised from the fall. Instinctively, he scrambled to his feet, raising his arms and desperately trying to take a breath. At first, it was impossible. He thought this might be the end. But with each attempt, a little more air managed to stick in his lungs. Still panicked, he stumbled around in the dark, gasping for air, and his hand struck a metallic object. Suddenly, he heard a rattling noise, and the dark room was flooded with bright light.

His eyes, still adjusted to the darkness, ached from the glaring light from all directions. He squeezed his eyes shut, then slowly and cautiously opened them. At first, he squinted through barely opened lids, then a bit more until he adjusted to the brightness. The sight nearly stopped his heart. Apparently, he'd triggered some sort of machinery. The room was now lit, revealing heavy, mysterious equipment producing crackling and humming sounds, with various gears coming to life. In a panic, he looked around the space.

The room was roughly 120 square meters, crammed with strange instruments he'd never seen before. On the walls were several warning signs with pictograms and plaques in old German script reading, "Caution: High Voltage!" He limped around, trying to make sense of where he'd ended up. He muttered to himself in disbelief, "No one's ever going to believe this." Fascinated yet terrified, he took in his surroundings. Lining the walls were cabinet-sized iron machines with dials and switches glowing and flashing in various colors, connected by arm-thick cables running across the room. He noticed a rusty, gray-painted iron door set into the wall between two pieces of equipment. It seemed these machines hadn't been in operation for years; many parts were corroded, some covered with a thick layer of dust. Mechanical parts squeaked, but each unit still functioned independently.

Scattered across the four corners of the room were various consoles with levers and antennas. But the most striking feature was at the center: a round platform with three steps leading up to a black leather recliner. Thick copper cables were coiled around it like a giant spool. Gradually catching his breath, Lennart hobbled to the door and tried with all his strength to push and pull it, but it was firmly locked. Looking up along the wall to his left, he saw an air vent just below the ceiling—it must have been the spot where he'd fallen in. His shopping bag still lay at the spot where he'd landed.

He limped over, picked up the bag, and looked inside, surprised to find the water bottle intact. The bread and cheese must have cushioned the glass bottle from breaking. He took it out, twisted off the cap, and drank a few large gulps. After closing it, he carefully put it back in the bag. Everything hurt. His ribs and back ached from the fall, and he had a lump on the back of his head. His ankle was twisted, and insect bites from his hike through the woods stung all over his skin. He and his clothes were smeared with forest soil. But his biggest worry was that he was trapped in this strange, underground concrete lab, with the only exit being the air vent, a full two meters above him.

He tried pushing some of the machines toward the vent to create a makeshift staircase, but they were so heavy he couldn't budge them an inch. He was simply too battered to be able to free himself from this dilemma. In desperation, Lennart shouted, "Hello? Is anyone there?" He saw no one, and no one answered.

Limping cautiously around the room, he inspected each machine closely, trying to guess their purpose. But the more he studied them, the less he understood. The design of these machines, the environment, and the lettering on the signs all suggested this might be an old Nazi bunker. And that strange recliner in the center could only have been part of some insane experiment. The constant mechanical sounds made his nerves raw, but he didn't dare switch off the lever he'd accidentally activated, preferring not to be plunged back into darkness.

Holding his shopping bag, he crept toward the center of the room, climbed the three steps to the platform, and skeptically examined the leather recliner. Suspended precisely above the chair, embedded in the concrete ceiling, was a massive copper coil. He cautiously wiped the dust from the chair with his hand, ready to bolt if anything happened. When nothing did, he sat carefully on the recliner, hoping to gather his thoughts, take a breather, and grasp the gravity of his situation.

The working machines generated a lot of heat, bringing the room to a comfortable temperature. The lounge chair was actually quite cozy and ergonomic. The armrests were soft, and the headrest was cushion-like. His entire body ached, so he decided to rest a little to regain his strength. He lay back and set his bag down on his chest. Lennart was so exhausted that, despite the loud rumbling of the machines, he fell into a deep sleep immediately. The entire day had been nerve-racking. In his sleep, he mumbled mostly unintelligible sounds, but now and then, fragments could be heard: "Nazis… They're Nazis!" He tossed and turned, his head and arms moving restlessly.

On the front part of the right armrest, there was a small black toggle switch. Without realizing it, his right hand slid it down. The machines started working even more intensely, and an unpleasant, high-pitched wail filled the air, ripping Lennart rudely from his sleep. Just as he wanted to leap up, a vortex of light began to swirl around him. Paralyzed with fear, he remained seated in the chair. The light grew ever stronger, and the shrill noise became unbearable. The room began to shake. The

whirlwind of light moved closer and closer until Lennart was completely engulfed in it. All he could do was let out a long, loud scream.
"Ahhhhh…" Above him, a bright funnel formed, directly beneath the copper coil embedded in the ceiling. With tremendous force, Lennart was sucked upward into the funnel. It felt as if all his cells were being stretched and pulled, as if he were being drawn out like spaghetti, meters long. Yet his mind remained alert. The movement through this tunnel of blinding light lasted only a few seconds. Terrified, he squeezed his eyes shut, convinced he'd just died.

Then, suddenly, everything felt different—quieter. Lying on his back as if drugged, Lennart slowly opened his eyes. What he saw looked surreal: an orange sky with bands of clouds drifting slowly overhead. In the faint distance, but overwhelmingly huge, he saw a majestic turquoise moon, so close he could see every crater and ridge with the naked eye. And next to this moon, a smaller, silvery one. Lennart had never seen anything so beautiful. "Aha! So this is what it's like when you die," he whispered to himself. He was entirely calm now. The sky was decorated with large and small stars in constellations he didn't recognize. A gentle breeze brushed over his face.

A bit dazed, he lifted his head and looked around. Amazed but still groggy, he noticed he was lying outdoors in what looked like a park, a little way from a large city, on a circular metallic surface. His shopping bag still rested on his chest. "Hmm. I guess I'm not actually dead. Or have I taken my silly groceries into the afterlife with me?" he muttered in confusion. With the back of his right hand, he casually brushed the bag aside. It fell to his left, and the bread slipped out. The water bottle slowly rolled out too, stopping when it hit the loaf of whole-grain bread. He looked off into the distance, seeing many tall buildings of an unfamiliar design. One structure, in particular, stood out—a church-like building shimmering in silver, encased in a half-dome of glass, with a spire-like peak emerging from the dome.

The façade was covered with beautiful ornamental designs, perfectly harmonious. But at the top of the spire, instead of a cross, there stood an elegant and proud giant metallic statue, polished to a high sheen, in a victorious pose, watching over the entire city. The figure looked somewhat strange; it was humanoid but not quite human, with a body shape and limb proportions that seemed just a little off. Lennart guessed this building must be at least 500 meters tall, reaching into the orange sky. In the distance, he noticed what looked like floating cars, moving with incredible speed but in complete silence across the skyline.

His body felt heavier than usual, as though he weighed almost twice as much. Breathing was difficult, like he was on a high mountain. It reminded him of stories from climbers who'd ascended thousands of meters above sea level. The air was thin; he really needed an oxygen mask. He felt too weak to get up and simply lay there, motionless. Gradually, his strength started to ebb away again. Lennart's attention faded; he grew weaker and soon slipped back into unconsciousness.

In a flash of fragmented images, he saw figures moving frantically, leaning over him and gesturing. Everything looked blurred and hazy. Then he blacked out again.

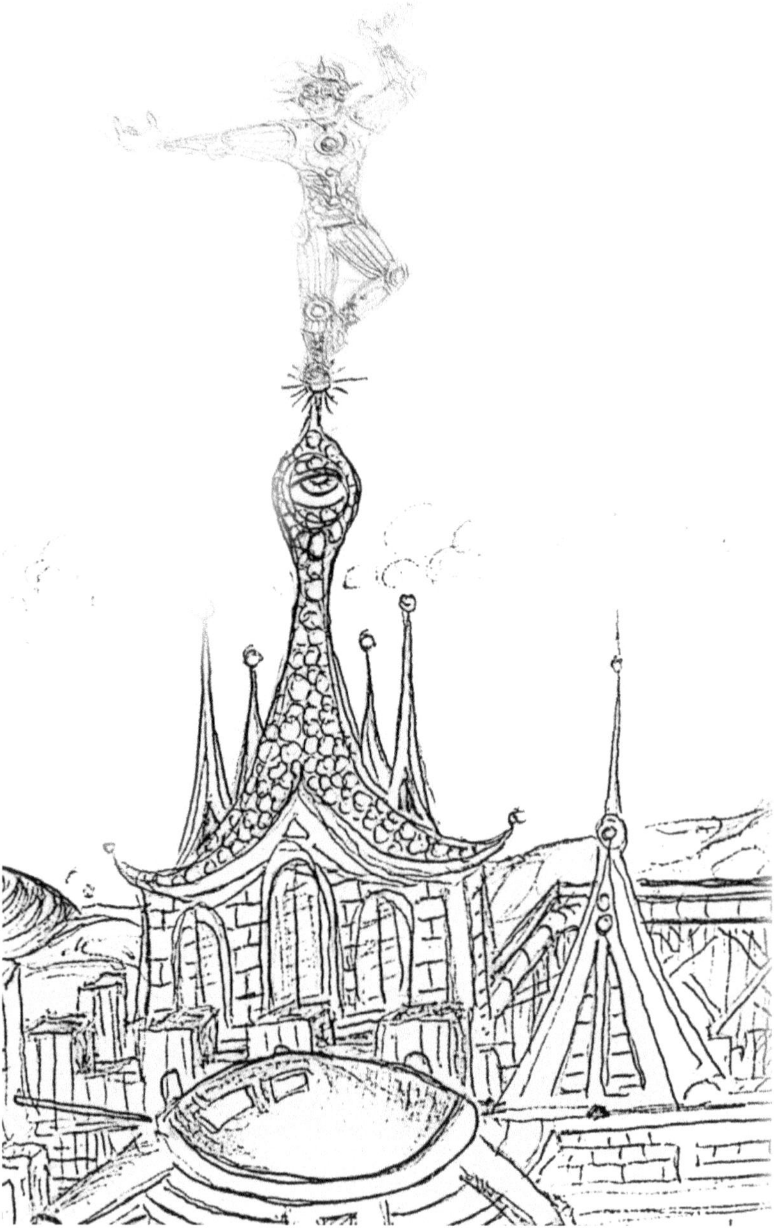

The next day, Felix was at work, still mulling over Lennart's last words. None of it made sense. Lennart had told him he would check in later, but since then his phone had been off the whole time. Felix struggled to focus on his tasks. Throughout the day, he tried calling Lennart several times but only reached his voicemail. Felix couldn't shake the uneasy feeling that something must have happened. He decided to call Lennart's parents during his lunch break and searched online for their phone number. Unfortunately, they weren't listed anywhere, so he had no choice but to keep waiting. The worry gnawed at him all day, making the hours drag by. Finally, work was over. Felix got into his car and drove to Lennart's place. Once there, he looked around the street but didn't see Lennart's car parked anywhere near the building. Felix rang the doorbell repeatedly at the entry intercom, nervously waiting for about fifteen minutes. There was no response, nothing at all. It was all very strange.

Images began to play in Felix's mind: Lennart was a true digital native, and for him to go so long without his phone, without any contact, was completely out of character. Under the circumstances, Felix couldn't help but think the worst, even though he was usually an optimist. Worried, he drove home. "Well," he told himself, trying to stay calm, "he'll probably call me tonight, and all this fuss will turn out to be nothing." With that, he headed home. Once there, he kept calling Lennart sporadically, but every time, it went straight to voicemail. The night passed without Lennart returning his call. Felix kept waking up, unable to sleep soundly. At dawn, he tried calling Lennart again, only to find that his phone was still off. So he got dressed, skipped breakfast, and headed to the nearest police station. He felt he had no choice but to report Lennart missing. There was no way he could find him on his own, and Lennart could be in real trouble.

Felix entered the station. The floor had just been polished. He headed directly to a small, glass-paneled information counter. A bored-looking officer pushed aside a small sliding window so they could talk. "How can I help you?" asked the officer. Felix, clearly agitated, replied, "Look, I haven't seen my friend Lennart Neumann for two days now. His phone's been off, he's not at home, and I'm really starting to worry!" The officer leaned back in his chair, unperturbed, and said in a flat tone, "Maybe Mr. Neumann just went on a trip or needed some time alone?" Felix, growing increasingly anxious, replied, his voice rising, "Listen! That's completely impossible. Lennart and I are in contact every day. The last thing he said to me was that he'd call later, and he usually keeps his word. Plus, he's more of a lone wolf; he wouldn't have anyone to visit." Finally, the officer shifted in his seat. "Well, then, talk to my colleagues. Down the hall, Room 5a. Maybe they can help you out." Felix thanked him and followed the directions.

In the designated room, an overweight officer sat behind his desk. Without missing a beat, Felix repeated the whole worrisome story. This officer listened with interest, asking questions about Lennart's habits, his personal details, his family, and his social circle. He then asked Felix to send him a recent photo of Lennart via email from his phone. Felix's contact information was also recorded. The officer then began typing everything into the computer with intense focus, as if in a race with the keyboard. After five minutes of furious typing, the printer whirred to life and printed out the missing persons report in duplicate. Felix received a copy, while the other was filed. The officer finally said, in a reassuring tone, "Most missing persons end up returning on their own. If that happens, please let us know. Otherwise, we'll start looking and will contact you as soon as we learn anything." Felix felt reassured that he'd done the right thing, thanked the officer, and left the station.

In a rush, he made his way to his car, knowing he needed to get to work quickly. He carefully folded the missing persons report and slipped it into his pocket. Taking a deep breath, he started the engine and sped off.

3. Habitat

Lennart's eyes flew open in an instant. He was lying on an incredibly comfortable, hammock-like lounge chair, with a soft mattress beneath him. Energized, he jumped to his feet and took a deep breath. Thankfully, he could breathe normally again. Miraculously, all his aches and pains had vanished—his back, his ribs, his head, even his left ankle were now pain-free. Looking down, he noticed he was dressed in a white robe. Examining his arms and hands, he saw that all his scratches and mosquito bites were gone.

He had no idea what time it was or how long it had been since his car broke down. Looking around, he murmured in confusion, "Where the hell am I?" He was inside a large, elongated, half-glass cylinder that curved up at the top. The glass was frosted and tinted. The cylinder stretched about four meters in radius and around thirty meters in length.

At eye level, every five meters along the glass walls, screens were embedded. These screens followed the curve of the walls, perfectly flush and seamless with the glass. Each screen displayed the outline of a human figure with blinking, ever-changing symbols that Lennart couldn't decipher. They seemed to be tracking his vital signs, including his heartbeat and brain activity, as the symbols near the head and chest changed most frequently.

Running the length of the cylinder's ceiling was a rounded metal panel, about 80 cm wide, with long ventilation slits cut into it. Through the slits, rotating fans of an air-conditioning system could be seen every few meters, moving slowly. A calming music—a blend of whale songs and harp notes—drifted softly from the ceiling. He could also hear a faint trickling of water from the back of the room.

Next to his lounge chair stood a small, rectangular metal cabinet with rounded corners. On top of it lay his jeans, his cotton shirt, his underwear, and socks—all neatly folded, perfectly pressed, and stacked. His phone, keys, and wallet, which had all been in his pockets, rested on top, stacked like the Bremen Town Musicians. Beside the cabinet, on the floor, sat his crumpled shopping bag and his sneakers.

Further ahead, the room was lushly adorned with plants, creating a paradise-like atmosphere. It looked as though a florist had spent hours arranging them. At each end of the cylinder stood silver metal walls with half-round doors equipped with turning knobs. The floor was covered with narrow, elegant wood-grain tiles that looked like rare rainforest hardwood—one that, for environmental reasons, shouldn't be used anymore. The flooring was lined with warm, amber-colored light that glowed gently from below.

Barefoot, Lennart walked slowly toward the center of the room, passing the decorative plants, until he reached a desk with a silver metal surface. To the left sat a conical glass carafe filled with water, beside a small empty bowl—likely for drinking. There was also a tablet or monitor on the desk, displaying those incomprehensible symbols. To the right of the monitor was a wooden cutting board, holding a selection of beautiful, yet unfamiliar fruits.

A stool stood in front of the desk, made of twisted, interwoven legs of wood that looked as if they had grown that way naturally. It was crafted from the same rare wood as the floor. To the left of the desk stood a miniature fountain shaped like a tree, carved from the same wood. Water trickled down its branches, creating a small waterfall. Lennart could easily place the water carafe underneath to fill it if he got thirsty.

The tasteful decor impressed him. He heard another, even softer trickling sound coming from the far end of the room, likely from behind the metal wall with the half-round door. Lennart felt relieved that he'd evidently been found, perhaps seriously injured, and brought here. He assumed he was now in a private clinic, somewhere upscale.

He wanted to talk with the staff, maybe a doctor, to understand his situation. "Surely, the nurses are bustling around the halls," he thought. Feeling intact and healthy, he decided to take a short walk outside this futuristic recovery room to speak with someone in the hallway. Curiosity overtook him; he was eager to find out what was behind that wall where the water was trickling. So he moved forward, right up to the door, reached out, and gripped the knob. Slowly, Lennart opened the door.

The sound of running water grew louder. He peeked through the doorway, and all he could say was a long, drawn-out, "Woooow."

It was an incredible sight—a room about 50 square meters in size, resembling the most beautiful waterfall he could ever have imagined. Plants, rounded, colorful stones, and crystals covered every surface. Water flowed from the very top, not just streaming down but cascading over the stones and flowers, forming miniature waterfalls. The air was filled with the rich scent of flowers, and the water foamed and splashed down onto a polished crystal floor. In essence, it looked like the most elaborate and stunning shower imaginable.

Next to the crystal floor was a large, cylindrical crystal stone, hollowed out on the inside.

The crystal cylinder was filled almost to the top with water, bubbling like a spring. Since it ended right at seat height, it could only be a toilet with a built-in bidet. "Wow, I can't imagine how much it must have cost to build a waterfall shower like this—and who even has the kind of imagination to design something this beautiful?" he thought, peeking through the door, awestruck and still. He felt an urge to step under the fragrant waterfall and refresh himself after all he had been through.

Opposite this beautiful bathroom was another door, perhaps leading to the hallway or a shared bathroom connected to an adjacent room. Lennart walked directly to this door and knocked three times, cautiously. All he wanted was to get home as soon as possible, and he was hoping to speak with a doctor. He was feeling fine now. He also wanted to find someone who could lend him a phone charger for a bit so he could reach Felix and check in on his online businesses. When no one responded to his knock, he turned the handle and quietly opened the door. He stepped inside cautiously and found a room identical to the first, only reversed.

"Hello? Is someone there?" he called out. He slowly made his way to the center of the room. Toward the far end, he saw another reclining chair, just like the one in the other room. Then, he noticed movement. Lennart spoke carefully: "Sorry to disturb you. I'm looking for…"

Suddenly, an elderly man with gray hair leaped from the chair, grasped his head, and stared at Lennart as if he were seeing a ghost. Lennart spoke to him again, in the same calm tone: "Please forgive me for disturbing you." But before he could finish, the old man interrupted, "Hallelujah, I've waited so long! Finally, finally, finally! A human! And he speaks German! Hooray! You've come on behalf of the Führer, to take me back home."

The man, who looked well over 90, was also dressed in white. He wobbled a bit but moved toward Lennart with surprising determination. Lennart stepped back, instantly sensing that the man was likely mentally ill. He didn't know how to handle this situation at all.

Uncertain, he addressed the trembling old man coming closer: "Listen, please, I'm sure this is just a misunderstanding. You must be mistaking me for someone else." The old man stopped just in front of Lennart and continued in the same ecstatic manner, "It's me, Eugen—Eugen Friedrich." He then wrapped his arms around Lennart as if they were lifelong friends. Lennart, embarrassed, took another step back and said, "Mr.

Friedrich, please don't take this the wrong way, but I don't know you at all. The reason I'm here is that I need to speak with a doctor or nurse. Please don't let me bother you."

"You can call me Eugen," replied the obviously confused old man, who went on: "My boy—you're German, and you were sent here on the Führer's orders to finally take me home!" Eugen danced a little and moved to his dresser, as if beginning to pack his belongings. Then he paused, lowered his voice, and whispered, "We have to be discreet, or Abron, the Zookeeper, will come and stop our escape!"

"Right, I get it," thought Lennart to himself. Clearly, he had ended up in some sort of mental institution. Why had they taken him to an asylum? He only had some bruises and sprains! It was obvious he needed to talk to a doctor urgently. With a touch of exasperation, he said, "Please listen to me, Mr. Friedrich. I was rescued from an old Nazi bunker after my car broke down. Your Führer went down in history as a coward, and Germany fortunately lost the Second World War in 1945. I wasn't sent by anyone, and I don't even know who you are."

Eugen stood still, appearing as if he had finally understood Lennart. "What Nazi bunker?" Eugen asked, his voice insistent. The old man's shoulders slumped in disappointment, as though he were just now realizing that his beloved Third Reich had been left in ruins. He continued, "My boy, you don't seem to realize where you've ended up. I'll prove what I'm telling you."

Eugen lowered his voice again and whispered, "I also ended up in that bunker back then, as a young orphan. It was top secret, part of the Fort Hahneberg facility. The goal was to establish contact with other worlds and obtain advanced technology for warfare. So, in 1944, they transported me here as a teenager, like some test subject, against my will. They promised they'd come back for me soon. They brought me here...to this zoo. Since then, I've tried countless times to escape and get back home, but Abron, the Zookeeper, always dragged me back."

Lennart's face twisted in disbelief, but he let Eugen continue.

"And now, what I'm about to tell you is going to sound terrible." Eugen paused and then went on, lowering his voice to almost a whisper, "We're on another planet. There's no way out because the environment isn't suited for humans. Only here, inside our capsules, can we survive. I'll prove it to you as promised. We are far, far from home, and no one knows that we're here. We're prisoners in an intergalactic zoo, where all kinds of species from everywhere are collected and observed. They give you food and everything you need, but leaving? That's impossible."

Lennart put on an expression that suggested he was listening intently, though he only crossed his arms and responded with a know-it-all tone, "And how exactly do you plan to prove this to me?" Eugen continued, "Poor boy, you don't believe me, do you? I'll prove it to you very simply, but brace yourself!"

Slowly, he walked to the frosted, half-curved glass wall, where monitors were built in just as in Lennart's room. He spread his hand flat on the curved glass and looked at Lennart with a worried expression. Gradually, the entire frosted pane cleared up. It lost its opacity and became fully transparent in a matter of seconds. Eugen, still keeping his hand on the glass, said, "Look closely. You'll probably see nothing else for the rest of your days but this."

What Lennart saw took his breath away. Long half-cylindrical glass tubes stretched to the left and right in parallel rows, creating long corridors between them. Nearly two-meter-tall, humanlike, extremely muscular beings in white robes strode through the corridors, glancing curiously into the glass tubes. Some of these beings had dark red-violet skin, while others were a pinkish color. Their faces were covered with strange, yet beautifully patterned ridges along the forehead and cheeks, forming naturally ornate lines around the mouth and eyes. Their noses were simply two slits positioned in the center of their faces, and their large, glowing green eyes gave them a watchful look.

The half-tubes seemed to have no visible beginning or end and held even stranger creatures within. Lennart's heart raced, and he began to sweat in excitement, yet he stood frozen, mouth half-open, eyes wide with shock. Eugen removed his hand from the glass, but the pane remained transparent. Almost as if detached from reality, he said in a monotone, "The pink-faced ones are females; the purple ones are males. They actually don't harm anyone. Even when I tried to escape several times, they continued to care for me without punishment. They always bring us these fruits to eat. They're actually quite tasty, except for one kind that's so horribly bitter I've refused to eat it since the beginning."

Lennart looked up along the metal strip that ran alongside the air conditioning vent through an outer glass pane. An orange sky and a large turquoise moon were visible. "When I was lying in the park, staring up at the sky, I thought at first that I must have died. But then, what I saw was actually real," he whispered.

"Of course, my boy!" Eugen responded. "Right on schedule, twice a day, Abron comes by, brings food, and checks on us. They must live forever here, because for as long as I can remember, Abron hasn't aged a day." Eugen spread his hand on the glass again, and the pane turned frosted once more. "Even though I've reactivated the screen, they can still see us from the outside. The only place with any real privacy is under the waterfall."

The old man came close to Lennart and quietly asked him, "I have so many questions. How is it back on Mother Earth? How are the people? What year is it? Who rules Germany? I've spent my whole life here, and I can't even imagine what it's like to walk freely outside, doing as one pleases. What wouldn't I give for a grilled chicken with roasted potatoes. I vaguely remember the crispy skin—I used to love that back in the orphanage; they'd give it to us at the beginning of each month. Tell me, friend!"

And so, the two talked for hours about Earth, science, politics, and good food. Lennart casually asked if it was difficult to escape from this place. The frail old man pointed to the door across from the waterfall shower on the other side of the room. "The doors aren't locked. You'll find yourself in a little chamber that works like an airlock. If you place your hand on the screen, the door to freedom will open. But know that you won't last long out there. There's too little air to breathe, and the gravity will get to you. They know that here, which is probably why they don't even bother locking the doors. Plus, they use the chambers themselves to come in and check on us. These beings have muscles like steel; they can walk around normally, but we tire quickly."

Lennart excused himself, saying he needed a moment to process it all and promised to return later. He made his way back through the bathroom into his own room. He stopped at the carafe of water, poured himself a cup, and drank slowly at first, then drained the cup in a few big gulps. He then approached the curved glass wall and placed his hand on the pane. In his room, too, the glass cleared, and he stood motionless, like a statue, looking out. First to the left, then to the right, and finally up, he examined the alien beings intensely. Some stopped in front of his pane, watching him with interest for a while before moving on. Others strolled by without even a glance.

He fell into deep thought. How could he live here? He couldn't accept existing as an attraction, like an animal in a zoo. Escape plans were already beginning to form in his mind.

He just had to find a way back to that park—the spot where he had first awoken on this strange planet. But how could he pull that off? Lost in thought, he suddenly heard the round door beside his cot open.

A muscular creature entered, dressed in a white protective suit that looked like something out of a futuristic rugby match. In one powerful, violet-toned hand, the male creature carried a large, roughly woven basket brimming with various fruits. A white breathing mask covered the area above his nostrils, with thin, white tubes running from it back to a sort of jetpack on his back. It was clearly some kind of breathing apparatus, though his mouth remained uncovered. He placed the basket on the metal table next to the small tower of Lennart's personal belongings. Then, in a loud, booming voice, he declared, "ABRON," pounding both fists against his armored chest. Lennart would have wet himself with fear if he had been wearing pants.

Cautiously, he placed his own hand on his chest and timidly said, "Lennart." Abron then slowly bowed, much like a customary gesture in many Asian cultures. Lennart's knees shook like leaves in the wind, but he pulled himself together, got up, and imitated the bow as best he could. Abron reached his long, muscular arm into the basket and took out a fruit that looked like a large, dark red, hairy kiwi. He spoke in his bass voice, "Mi schuk do amam di ruck. Asam mi kudlahrah ULAM." Then he hissed through his pale pink teeth, eyeing Lennart as if evaluating him. Abron then laughed like a villain, waved dismissively, knowing full well that Lennart didn't understand a word, turned, and exited the room exactly as he had entered.

Lennart's throat felt as dry as desert sand. His heart raced. This was nothing like how he had imagined an encounter with extraterrestrials. His physiological state was clearly displayed on the medical monitors attached to the wall. The human figure on the screen blinked, and incomprehensible symbols near the chest area kept changing color. Lennart's stomach hurt with hunger, so he quickly ate a few banana-like fruits that tasted sweet and were quite filling. He saved the rest for later, then put his hand on the glass wall again to activate the opaque privacy shield. To calm himself, he decided to lie down for a moment. He needed time to process everything he had just experienced. "This can't be real! Eugen was right about every word. And at first, I thought he was completely insane," he thought to himself.

After a while, lying down had helped him calm down. The soothing harp music and whale songs returned his heartbeat to a steady rhythm. He knew he needed to go back to Eugen to learn everything he could about these creatures. One thing was certain: he had to escape as soon as possible. Determined, he walked through the waterfall shower and knocked on Eugen's door. "Come in, my boy," came a quiet voice from the other side. Lennart entered Eugen's room and headed straight to the cot where Eugen lay, staring up with a serious expression.

"Am I disturbing you?" Lennart asked cautiously. "I can come back later." Eugen shook his head. "I've been alone in this place my whole life, talking to the walls. It's good to have someone here to exchange a word with—comrade," he said, his voice slightly trembling as if he already sensed that Lennart wasn't planning to stay long. "I just met Abron earlier. That guy is built like a tank. Man, was I trembling," Lennart said, standing on his tiptoes and puffing out his chest in a comical imitation of Abron's massive figure. "Then he said something I didn't understand. Something with 'ULAM.' Do you understand their language?"

Eugen shook his head again and replied, "I don't understand much of it, but I know 'ULAM.' It's that disgusting-tasting fruit. They keep trying to make us eat it, so I suppose it's important to them that you eat that weird bitter thing too." Lennart scratched his head, puzzled by the strange hiss Abron made when he spoke of the fruit. Then he continued questioning Eugen: "How is this planet structured? When is it night here? How many hours are there in a day? Is it anything like Earth?"

Without answering any of his questions, Eugen simply said, "Boy, I've tried to escape many times but never succeeded. Now I feel my life slipping away, and I know my time is near. If you manage to do what I couldn't… I mean, if you make it back home, you'll find this useful." He tugged at a leather cord around his neck. A single rusty key hung from it. He removed it and handed it to Lennart, saying, "This is the key to freedom. I don't need it anymore." Then he waved Lennart off and said, "I'm tired. Come back some other time."

Without asking any more questions about what kind of freedom the key might open up, Lennart took it, nodded at the old man with understanding, and quietly returned to his room. Once inside, he lay down and started planning his escape. He deactivated the screen shielding to check if night had finally fallen. No more alien visitors were wandering curiously through the corridors. Through the glass ceiling of his room, he could see that the sky had indeed darkened. After thinking things over, he slept briefly, maybe an hour.

When he woke, he got dressed, took his purchases out of the bag on his dresser, then brought the empty bag and his clothes into the shower. He stripped off the tunic he'd been wearing and took a long shower. Refreshed, he put his own clothes back on, took the bag, and spread it open, waving it around to capture as much air as possible. He then twisted the top closed, gripping it in his fist, making an airtight seal. His plan was to alternate between breathing from the bag and from the outside air. This way, he imagined, if the park wasn't too far, he could make it back home.

Bag in hand, he reentered his room, methodically placing his phone, keys, and wallet into his pockets. He slipped the leather cord with the key around his neck. Taking a few deep breaths, he held his breath, placed his hand on the door monitor leading to the pressurized exit, and then the door opened. He instantly felt the gravity of the planet press down on him. But he pressed on, marching quickly down the hallway, which stretched out about 200 meters in front of him. Along both sides were cylindrical glass rooms with bizarre creatures within. Some were very active, and each species had entirely different interior designs in their rooms. Without wasting any time, Lennart continued forward, holding his breath as long as possible, sometimes breathing from the bag, other times from the surrounding air. Each breath, he held his breath again.

The end of the hallway came into view, and he started to sweat. His legs felt the onset of fatigue, but he pushed on. At last, he reached the end of the hall, where six corridors branched off in a star pattern, each hosting its own alien beings. In the center was a cylindrical glass shaft split down the middle: on one side, elevators descended continuously, like a paternoster lift, while on the other side they rose. Looking up, Lennart could barely believe his eyes—twelve floors above him and two floors below, each branching off like this one.

He stepped into a descending elevator, hopping off at the very bottom floor. Continuing with his breathing plan, alternating with the bag and holding his breath, he noticed that breathing the planet's air was becoming harder. Resolute, he struggled onward toward the glass exit doors. They opened automatically as he approached. Nervously, he looked around; the alien beings were everywhere, moving about in their white robes. They watched Lennart with astonishment, some even following at a cautious distance. He had no idea which direction to go but remembered the giant building with the victory statue. But he couldn't see it anywhere. Other towering structures, equally impressive, might have been blocking the view.

Time was running out. The air in his bag was almost gone. Growing frantic, he was consuming more oxygen, his muscles burning with exhaustion. His mind clouded as he ran in random directions, his vision fading. He collapsed to the ground, and then everything went dark. He had lost consciousness.

4. Hope

Meanwhile, Felix was deeply absorbed in his work when his phone rang. The caller ID displayed an unfamiliar landline number that he didn't recognize. Still focused on his work, he answered: "Hello, this is Felix speaking." On the other end, a police officer introduced himself as Officer Schmidt. "You filed a missing person report yesterday. Has your friend shown any signs of contact since then?"

With a somber tone, Felix replied, "No, I call several times a day. All I get is his voicemail." The officer continued, "There's been a development. We found Mr. Lennart Neumann's abandoned vehicle in a wooded area near Staaken, by Berlin. It appears his car may have broken down. We're planning to comb through the area with colleagues and search dogs as soon as the paperwork is approved. Hopefully, the scent trail from the car will be enough—unless you have a personal item of Mr. Neumann's, like a piece of clothing. The vehicle we found is locked, unfortunately. And the weather's against us: according to the forecast, a warm thunderstorm is brewing in the area, so if we're unlucky, we won't be able to do much with the dogs."

Felix was speechless for a moment, his mind racing through worst-case scenarios. He thought for a second, then responded, "Unfortunately, I don't have anything of his. I don't even have a key to his apartment to get you something." His voice remained heavy with sadness. The officer asked him to take down his number, just in case he thought of anything else. "We've contacted Mr. Neumann's parents," the officer added. "They're already on their way to Berlin, and they do have a key." He thanked Felix for the information, saying they'd stay in touch.

After hanging up, Felix slumped in his chair, took a deep breath, picked up his phone, and called Nicole. "Hi Nicole, it's Felix. Something might really have happened to my friend Lennart. The police just called; they found his car abandoned near some woods. They're planning to search the area." Nicole, moved by sympathy, replied gently, "That's awful. I can't imagine how you must feel. Let me know if there's anything I can do to help."

Felix wanted to ask her a favor, but wasn't sure how to phrase it without sounding too needy or leaving a poor impression on her. He stammered, struggling to get the words out: "Well... um, I mean... maybe if... it'd be easier if... so I wouldn't be alone..." Confused, Nicole asked, "Do you want us to meet? Would you like to talk?"

This prompt was just what Felix needed to finally say what was on his mind. "Yes, exactly. I'd like to go with you to Staaken and look for Lennart's car. The police will probably tow it soon anyway. I don't want to go alone, but I'd understand if you're not up for it." Nicole asked, puzzled, why he'd want to go there at all. Felix hesitated before replying, "I wanted to... I thought... I'd just like to see it for myself. The officer didn't tell me much over the phone, and I wasn't expecting the call, so I didn't really ask any questions."

Nicole paused for a few seconds, then reluctantly agreed, though she doubted the point of driving around aimlessly in such a vast area looking for an abandoned car. Felix suddenly felt uneasy. He realized it might not have been such a good idea to ask her for this favor. She didn't seem to understand what he was going through. He quickly decided to go alone. To Nicole, he said, "You're right, it was just a thought. Let's leave it to the police and wait to hear what they find." He wished her a good day and agreed to talk again soon. He ended the awkward conversation as quickly as possible.

As much as he'd enjoyed getting closer to her a few days earlier, Felix realized now how superficial it all felt. Nicole was kind, but he was alone in his worry. "What an idiot I am! Why did I even ask her?" he muttered to himself. Negative thoughts flooded his mind. What if Lennart was injured somewhere, fighting for his life? Or what if he'd been attacked in the woods and killed? He could barely stand his own thoughts. The hours dragged on in slow motion. He counted down the minutes until he could leave work. Shortly before the end of his shift, he filled out a vacation request form, went to his supervisor's office, and asked for three days off on short notice for personal reasons. His boss could see the worry on Felix's face and sensed something was wrong, but refrained from asking further questions. He approved the request quickly, saying, "I hope it's nothing serious." He asked Felix to set up an out-of-office message and brief his nearby colleague on his current tasks just in case.

Once he'd done everything to his boss's satisfaction, Felix headed home. There, he made himself something to eat and sat down at his computer. Grabbing a notepad, he began researching, trying to narrow down the area where Lennart's car was most likely located. He spent hours on it, planning his route late into the night.

The scrap paper was covered with street names and sketches. Felix was dog-tired. With his last bit of strength, he managed to turn off the computer, then dragged himself to bed with difficulty. Within minutes, he was deeply asleep. It rained throughout the night until morning. The next day, Felix quickly jumped into the shower, carelessly slapped a few slices of salami onto two pieces of bread, and devoured them in large bites without really chewing. He got dressed in the meantime, sat down next to his computer where his notes lay, and programmed his phone's navigation based on his planned route. As soon as he was done, he headed out toward his car. On the way, he made a quick stop at the bakery to grab a coffee to go.

Felix got into his car, switched on the navigation, and set off at a leisurely pace. Forty-five minutes later, he reached Staaken. He slowed down, looking around carefully. Other cars impatiently passed him, honking, as he was driving too slowly for their liking. But unfazed, Felix kept his slow speed, making sure he didn't miss Lennart's abandoned car. He even drove down completely deserted paths, taking a whole hour to cover his planned route without spotting the car. He retraced certain forest paths twice. Slowly, doubts crept in about whether he would find the vehicle at all. He had covered about 95 percent of the route. Just as he was about to give up, he saw a car parked about 200 meters ahead by the roadside. The closer he got, the more certain he was that it was Lennart's car.

Excited, he parked behind the abandoned vehicle. He immediately recognized the warning triangle on the rear shelf. He got out and inspected the car from all sides. There was no sign of any violence—no dents, no scratches. He cupped his hands around his face to peer through the driver's window. The interior looked a bit messy, but that was normal; Lennart never bothered to vacuum after filling up the tank. Felix also examined the ground around and beneath the car, which was still damp from the rain, but there were no traces of blood. On the one hand, he felt a slight relief, but on the other, his friend was still missing without a trace.

Felix locked his own car and walked a little way into the forest, scanning for any obvious clues. When he found nothing unusual, he understood there wasn't much he could do to help. He also knew that the longer Lennart went without any sign of life, the less likely it was that he was still alive. Felix returned to his car, drank the now-cold coffee, and murmured sorrowfully, "Lenni, buddy, where are you? Just come back." At least, seeing Lennart's car in person gave him a small glimmer of hope that he might still be alive. Felix marked the car's location in his navigation, started the engine, and drove back home, feeling sad and still uncertain.

Slowly, Lennart's eyes opened. He was back in his room, once again dressed in the white gown. He heard the soft whale song, accompanied by the harp music. He sprang up from his bed. Fresh fruits sat on the silver dresser, neatly arranged beside all his things, stacked up again. He took one of each fruit from the bowl. Some could be eaten with the skin, while others needed peeling. He examined the fruit Abron Ulam had told him about, peeled it, and took a cautious bite, wincing immediately. "Ugh, that tastes awful," he muttered with a grimace. It tasted sour and unripe, with a nasty, bitter aftertaste. Quickly, he wiped his lips with his arm, trying to shake off the awful taste.

Disappointed by his failed escape attempt, Lennart took a waterfall shower. But he was also glad to be alive. He removed his white robe, leaving the leather strap with the key around his neck, and enjoyed the shower. Afterwards, he slowly got dressed and knocked on Eugen's door. No answer. He knocked again—nothing. No sound. Carefully, he opened Eugen's door, looked inside, and called, "Hello, Eugen, are you there?" The room was empty.

It dawned on him that there were only two possibilities. The first, and highly unlikely one, was that Eugen had attempted to escape. But everything pointed more to his death—the passing of the key to freedom, and his remark that his time had come. Lennart realized he was alone now. He felt a new weight of solitude, though he'd always been fine by himself. This, however, was a completely different kind of loneliness.

He returned through the shower room to his own quarters. Turning off the privacy screen, he observed his surroundings attentively and muttered, "There must be a way out of this habitat!" Then he lay back on his bed and clasped his hands together.

On the dresser next to his bed lay his groceries, unpacked. He picked up the cheese, looked at the packaging, and sniffed it. The cheese no longer looked appetizing, and the whole-grain bread had started to grow mold. He wanted to throw them away but couldn't find a trash can anywhere. So he put the slightly spoiled food back down indifferently. Reaching into the large fruit bowl, he ate everything except the bitter Ulam fruits.

He saw Abron standing beside the decompression chamber with a fresh fruit bowl, donning a breathing mask over his slitted nose. In seconds, Abron stood in the room, exchanged the fruit baskets, and noticed Lennart hadn't eaten the bitter Ulams. Picking up one of the fruits, he mimicked chewing on it, letting air hiss through his teeth as if to make a point. But when he saw that Lennart was staring back at him, like a frightened gazelle watched by a hungry predator, Abron gave up on his pantomime. He paused a moment, then turned to leave.

Lennart summoned all his courage and, with urgency, called out, "Eugen. Where is Eugen?" He pointed toward the neighboring room, trying to understand what had happened to him. Abron tilted his head to the side, closing his eyes briefly as if in thought, then looked up as if gazing toward the sky. He gave a sympathetic nod when he saw that Lennart understood his gesture as a confirmation of death.

Abron left the room, visibly satisfied. He stopped in front of Lennart's glass panel when he noticed a female inhabitant of the planet approaching. He removed his breathing mask and started conversing with her. Reaching into his nearly empty basket, he pulled out an Ulam fruit and showed it to her. Both looked at Lennart. Then she took the fruit from Abron's hand and approached the glass. She pretended to take a bite and chewed on thin air.

"Yeah, yeah," Lennart said indifferently, "your weird fruit tastes awful!" He lay down on his cot with resignation until the two of them left. His mind revolved around only one thought—how could he manage to get home again? He got up and started searching around. He must have lost his breathing bag when he passed out during his last escape attempt. He then began pacing the room like a scout, looking for anything useful, something that might aid his escape. Finding nothing, he proceeded through the shower room to Eugen's quarters.

"Maybe I'll find something in Eugen's things," he thought eagerly. On the dresser, he found a folded pocket knife and a closed pocket watch.

He carefully opened the watch. It had stopped, who knew how long ago. He also found Eugen's clothes, which he took with him just in case; he might find a use for them. He returned to his room and sat at the desk in the middle of the room to examine everything he had found. He opened the pocket knife, cautiously testing the blade's sharpness with his thumb. "Good, nice and sharp," he noted with satisfaction. Then he opened the pocket watch, studying the antique piece. The metal cover reflected his face, and by looking at his stubbly beard, he figured he'd been gone for at least three to five days. He inspected each piece of clothing carefully, checking every pocket for anything hidden. They were empty.

Could Eugen have been right? Lennart refused to accept the thought of spending the rest of his life in this glass habitat. Optimistically, he said to himself, "There has to be a way out, and I'll find it!" He placed Eugen's clothes on the dresser with his own things. He realized that if he wanted to return home, he'd need to train, to build up his stamina so he could make the trip across the park. Without wasting time, he began exercising, cycling through three exercises: push-ups, squats, and sit-ups, over and over until his muscles ached. He resolved to do these as often as possible.

Afterward, he took a shower. When he returned to his room, the female alien was once again standing outside the glass. With her palm pressed to the glass, she watched him curiously, holding another Ulam fruit in her other hand. Once again, she pantomimed eating the fruit. The whole situation was bizarre. Lennart wondered if the fruit might be some kind of national dish, something the aliens considered a polite offering for visitors—a delicacy by their standards. He thought briefly about this possibility, as he didn't want to offend anyone. So, he took an Ulam fruit from the basket, doing it slowly on purpose so the alien observing him could see exactly what he was doing. He peeled the hairy fruit, watching her reaction carefully. She genuinely seemed pleased. Then came the unpleasant part. Cautiously, he bit into the bitter fruit. Instantly, his eyes squeezed shut, and the corners of his mouth pulled down. He couldn't help but shudder at the horrible taste, his entire body jolting in reaction. He looked absurd. When he opened his eyes, he saw her clutching her belly in laughter from behind the glass.

"Great! At least one of us is having fun here," he muttered, feeling slightly annoyed. He put the fruit back in the basket. Still irritated, he lay back down on his cot, and soon after, she left, laughing to herself. Exhausted from training, Lennart drifted off to sleep.

Meanwhile, Felix was at home watching TV when his phone rang. It was that same landline number from the police. This time, he recognized it immediately and answered in a flurry of excitement. "Hello, this is Jörg Schmidt calling. It's about the search for your friend, Mr. Neumann. Unfortunately, our efforts haven't led to any results. Wherever Mr. Neumann is, he's definitely not in the forest area, or within several kilometers around his car," the officer informed him. "We're going to wind down the search shortly, though, of course, the case is still open. Next, we'll be sending the car to our experts. Forensics will take a closer look at the vehicle, and maybe they'll find something that can help us in the search." The officer's tone was reassuring as he continued, "Mr. Neumann's parents allowed us access to his apartment, and we used his scent as a reference for the search dogs. But the rain made it impossible for them to pick up any trail. We also asked them about places he might have gone—places he turned to as a child, locations he might have felt a longing for. No hints about his whereabouts, though." Felix was at a loss.

He couldn't understand the world anymore. Then he added one last thing to the officer: "Mr. Schmidt, if I can help in any way, you can always count on me. I've even taken a few days off, so I've got the time." Mr. Schmidt thanked him politely for the offer, and they said goodbye. For a moment, Felix thought of calling Nicole. But he quickly dismissed the idea. He was disappointed in her—not only because she hadn't done him the favor he'd asked for, but because she hadn't checked in since then. Not even a quick five-minute call to ask about his missing friend's situation. That would have shown some character.

Later, though, different thoughts came to him. He didn't want to judge her too harshly. Maybe he just wasn't as close or as important to her as he had assumed. He remembered something Lennart had once said about the girls he had dated: "The women I get involved with are like the black hole at the center of our galaxy. Always hungry for more, always consuming everything around them. And after devouring everything—even stars—it's as hungry as ever. And I'm supposed to keep feeding it to keep it happy?" Felix had always brushed off Lennart's remarks with a smile, but now he understood. He felt wounded inside. The unexplained disappearance of his best friend was weighing on him. He was in a weak moment.

In the end, he realized it wasn't really about women specifically. It felt like most people had been infected by a kind of global epidemic called selfishness. Outwardly, they were all a big, caring family of humans, but as soon as you looked closer, everyone was just their own best friend. Trying to take his mind off things, he turned on the TV for a while. The programs didn't lift his mood much—first, a report on rising poverty in Germany. A struggle for survival, just for a little money to get through each day. Once again, he thought of Lennart, who was scraping by, sacrificing so much, just because it was so hard to find the cash to cover the basics. Money that would immediately be spent on necessities. Living hand-to-mouth.

Then the news came on. One horror story after another. Murder and mayhem, all over the globe. It pulled him down so much that he decided to turn off the TV. He still couldn't clear his head, though, so he got up and got ready to go out. He got into his car, entered the coordinates where Lennart's car was found into the GPS, and set off.

The drive took over an hour, as he had to cut through rush-hour traffic. When he finally arrived, hearing the GPS announce, "You have arrived at your destination!" he saw that Lennart's car was being loaded onto a tow truck. Next to the tow truck driver stood a policeman, and they were talking. Felix parked his car right behind them, got out, and introduced himself briefly. He asked the policeman if he was Mr. Schmidt, and the officer confirmed it. Mr. Schmidt looked a little surprised and asked Felix how he had known where to find Lennart's car so precisely without being told. Mr. Schmidt's eyebrows furrowed thoughtfully.

Felix explained that the officer had mentioned on the phone that the car had been found abandoned on a wooded path in Staaken. From there, he had searched online, looking up various possible locations Lennart might have gone. He had been searching for quite a while, and just when he was about to give up, he finally found the car. The officer listened to Felix's explanation skeptically, handed him his business card, and asked him to come to his office for an appointment during his short vacation. Mr. Schmidt had to leave, as the car was now being transported to the station, and he urgently needed to be there. After that, everyone cleared out. The tow truck with Lennart's car drove away, followed by the officer. Felix was left standing alone at the edge of the woods.

He felt uneasy after this brief encounter. From Mr. Schmidt's behavior, he sensed that the officer found it suspicious how Felix had known exactly where the car was. He shook his head at the thought. On the one hand, he understood that they were grasping at every small clue. But he muttered to himself, "Well, I could've saved myself this whole trip." He did a 360-degree turn, taking in Lennart's last known location one more time. Then he got back into his car and drove home, deep in thought.

He barely slept at all that night. The next afternoon, completely overtired, he turned on the TV again. While it was on, he made himself a big salad in the kitchen. In summer, he couldn't eat anything heavy. He settled into his cozy armchair, with a big bowl of salad, watching TV as he ate until he was totally full. It wasn't until he finished that he realized he'd eaten way too much. He set the empty bowl aside, and, overwhelmed by the feeling of fullness, he fell into a deep sleep. At some point during the night, he woke up again. His neck hurt. Slightly grumpy, he went to bed, hoping to drift off again.

Just as he was about to fall back asleep, he was jolted awake by the doorbell. "Who's ringing at this hour?" he grumbled into the intercom. "Criminal police! Please open the door!" a voice echoed from the speaker. Adrenaline shot through Felix's body.

When he opened the door, a plainclothes man held up a metal badge on a chain in front of him. Behind him stood five more officers, who immediately filed into his apartment one after another. "Mr. Felix Schulte, you are under strong suspicion of being connected to the disappearance of your friend Lennart Neumann. Therefore, we have been ordered to search your apartment for possible clues," said the plainclothes officer, pulling a document from a clipboard. Felix, who was standing at the door in nothing but his underwear, was told to put on some clothes. Then he was instructed to sit in his living room chair and stay there, while one of the officers kept a constant eye on him to ensure he followed all instructions.

The other officers began turning his apartment upside down. He wasn't allowed to stand up. When one of the officers went to take his computer, he also found the rough notes Felix had taken while searching for Lennart's car. "Aha, now this is interesting! Looks like a plan. So you thought this whole thing through." He immediately called over several colleagues. "Mr. Schulte, unfortunately, due to the evidence we've found, we'll need to take you to the station for further questioning. Your shoes, your computer, your cell phone, and these notes will be taken in as evidence. All these items will be analyzed," said the plainclothes detective as the smaller items were placed into bags. The computer was put into a box and taken away. After that, the officer informed him of his rights. Then he was handcuffed and taken out. Felix said urgently, "For God's sake, you've got this all wrong. I can explain everything." He had no idea what was happening. He was taken to the station somewhat roughly.

There, they took his fingerprints and handprints, then placed him in a cell for several hours. While he sat alone in the cell, he mentally reviewed his situation and wondered what the police had against him that could lead to such drastic action. Had they found Lennart dead? But he had an alibi. At the time Lennart went missing, he'd been at a café with Nicole and Evelyn. He'd also left a message on Lennart's voicemail. The café staff could confirm he'd been there late into the evening. Eventually, he was taken to an interrogation room, where he sat alone again for quite a while until, at last, Mr. Schmidt entered the room with a stack of papers.

Mr. Schmidt sat down across from Felix, engrossed in his documents. "So, Mr. Schulte…" he said after a long pause, continuing, "…we believe you have something to do with Mr. Neumann's disappearance. We have here some rather serious pieces of evidence, and today I'll be asking you about them. On the driver's side window, we found your fingerprints. Then…" Mr. Schmidt paused again, leafing through his papers before continuing: "We also questioned your employer, who reported that in recent days, you seemed increasingly nervous and ultimately requested special leave for personal reasons. Then we found a note in your apartment that included the location of the car. In your computer's search history, we also identified that same location. When you arrived at the car without any directions, I ordered that all ground traces at the scene be analyzed. We found your shoe prints next to the abandoned vehicle and your tire tracks behind it. The primary reason we decided to arrest you was the suspicion that you may have gone to the scene to remove potential evidence. So, what did you do to Mr. Lennart Neumann?"

Felix, visibly frustrated, answered curtly, "Mr. Schmidt, let's get one thing straight. I was the one who reported Lennart missing. I spoke with him on the phone on the day he disappeared while he was at a post office in Berlin, and he promised to call me back, but he didn't. You can see that in my phone's call history. You can also check with Lennart's phone provider and see all my call attempts and the message I left on his voicemail. That same evening, I'd set up a meeting with two women, Nicole and Evelyn, at a café, because I wanted Lennart to join us. The meeting lasted late into the evening. When he became unreachable, I drove both girls home afterward. When his car was found, I researched on my computer where it could be and took some notes. On my own, after the heat storm, I went to check various places and left my footprints in the wet mud. I also leaned on the car window with both hands to look inside. But all this was after I filed the missing person report. Regarding my employer's statement, of course, it's true. How would you feel if your best friend went missing, and every day you lost more hope of ever seeing him again? Would you be able to just stay calm and work as usual without getting anxious? I can't do that!"

Mr. Schmidt took note of everything Felix had said and replied, "We'll look into this. Now, please provide us with the contact information for both women and the café's location." Once Felix wrote down all the information, he was returned to his cell.

5. Respiration

Lennart woke up on his cot, full of energy. He started his day with exercise. Although he had a bit of muscle soreness from yesterday's push-ups, he pushed through his routine tirelessly. Methodically, he cycled through push-ups, squats, and sit-ups until his muscles ached all over. His arms and legs were shaking. In the back of his mind, he focused solely on his escape, and nothing was going to stop him. He missed his shopping bag, which had provided him with enough air so he could step outside the habitat and even move around a little outdoors. He never would have thought that a shabby, crumpled shopping bag could mean so much to him.

Afterward, he took a waterfall shower. Freshly washed, he grabbed a bowl of fruit from the dresser and sat at the desk in the middle of the room. He moved the water carafe aside and pulled the fruit bowl close, picking out the tastiest fruits and savoring them. He hadn't turned his privacy screen on since he wanted to be aware of his surroundings as much as possible. He also didn't want to be caught off guard if someone entered his room. His internal clock told him that Abron should be coming soon with his meal. As he was busy peeling a few fruits, he didn't notice someone entering his room. When he finally realized, he was startled. Looking closely, he saw that it wasn't Abron but rather her — the female figure in a white protective suit.

He didn't know why, but he felt far less intimidated by her than by Abron. It seemed like she and Abron had coordinated because today, she was bringing him fresh fruit. She approached him slowly until she was standing right beside him. She tapped her chest plate with her free hand and said, "Zafina." Lennart mirrored her gesture, placing his hand on his chest and introducing himself, pronouncing his name slowly. Then, she bowed in a gesture of courtesy, just as Abron had done initially. Lennart returned the bow, acknowledging her greeting. She set down the full basket next to the one Lennart was eating from. To his surprise, she pulled a few items from the basket: a cutting tool similar to a paring knife, a mortar, and a pestle. She looked at him expectantly with her large, bright green eyes, as if waiting for a reaction.

Lennart mimed peeling a fruit, putting it in the mortar, and mashing it with the pestle. Zafina nodded approvingly. What was she planning? Was he supposed to eat mashed fruit for a change? She spoke to him in her language: "mi sepehegelu du kampkatschiri ULAM kaban." He nodded as if he understood but shrugged, still unsure why he was supposed to mash his fruit. The only thing that unsettled him was that word "Ulam" again. Why on earth did they insist he eat this fruit, even though it was so obviously unappealing, practically inedible to him?

Then, she placed her large, pink hand on Lennart's hair and gently stroked his head, somewhat like one would pet a dog. Lennart liked it. Her gaze was warm, almost loving. Surprised by the affection, he closed his eyes and enjoyed each touch. Then, she pulled the items closer to herself, took two Ulam fruits from the basket, peeled them, and placed them in the mortar. She also added two of the sweet, starfruit-like fruits and began mashing them with her strong hands, turning them into a pulp within minutes. She poured a little water from the carafe on the table and mixed everything thoroughly. A thick purple fruit blend emerged, reminding Lennart of Abron's skin color.

"A smoothie!" he said dreamily, looking skeptically at the result. His expression was unintentionally a mix of friendliness and disgust. She nodded slightly, then burst out laughing, clutching her hips as if in pain. Through her laughter, she managed to repeat, "SMUSI," echoing his word. She seemed to find it so funny that pink tears began rolling from her eyes. Her laughter was infectious, and Lennart joined in, both chuckling for several minutes. Finally, she indicated that he should drink the fruit mixture. She poured the entire contents of the mortar into a glass bowl by the water carafe, held it up, and handed it to Lennart. Zafina watched him expectantly.

He knew both flavors separately and figured that a mix of the two had to taste better than Ulam on its own. Cautiously, he took a small sip, smacking his lips as he tasted it. She started laughing loudly again. It actually tasted okay. Gathering his courage, he gulped down the entire bowl without pausing. He set the bowl down and asked, "Well, happy now? I ate your ULAM!" She clearly understood the word "ULAM," nodding in satisfaction and taking Lennart by the hand.

She led him to his cot, and they both sat down beside each other. She lifted her hand, holding her palm toward him as if to ask for a moment's patience. Lennart observed her up close without being obvious about it. He found her truly fascinating. That pink, flower-scented skin, those large, expressive green eyes, and the delicate ornaments around her sensory organs — he realized he actually liked Zafina. She exhibited so many human-like traits: the way she stroked his head, her delightful laughter. He appreciated it all deeply. And now he was finally about to learn what the mysterious Ulam fruit was all about.

Just a few minutes after finishing the bowl, Lennart's entire body began to tingle, as if a swarm of tiny ants were marching all over him from head to toe. It felt similar to when a foot "falls asleep" and then the blood starts rushing back, prickling and warming it. A bit alarmed, he pointed out to Zafina that something was changing in his body. The sensation quickly intensified, and his hands cramped up, clenching tightly into fists—so tight, in fact, that he couldn't open them with his own strength. Even his facial muscles tensed up around his mouth, pursing his lips together as if he were making a kiss. The tingling didn't let up, and Zafina took this as the signal she had been waiting for. She gently took him by the forearm, guiding him toward the room's exit.

Frightened by his body's reaction to the fruit, Lennart began to panic. When he realized Zafina wanted to lead him out of the room, his eyes went wide. The thought of stepping into the hostile outside environment made his mind recoil. But, inexplicably, he trusted her. She opened the door to the small decompression chamber, and they slowly stepped into the hallway that ran between the living quarters. They paused for a moment. Zafina removed her breathing mask, then put his arm over her shoulder to support him. Lennart could hardly believe his luck. He could actually breathe outside his glassed-in room.

After a few minutes, the cramps in his hands and around his mouth gradually released. Overjoyed, he gently patted her shoulder with the arm she was holding. Now able to speak a little, he asked, "Is this...the effect of ULAM?" She looked at him with a calm expression, nodded, and repeated, "ULAM—ULAM!" Together, they walked slowly down the hall. Lennart couldn't understand how this fruit allowed him to breathe in such thin air. "Maybe the ULAM fruit supplies my blood with enough oxygen," he mused. Still leaning on Zafina, they moved slowly along the corridor as Lennart curiously examined the habitats of the other life forms housed there.

Directly across from his room, there lived a humanoid bird-like creature. It had the physique of an orangutan, but instead of fur, its body was covered in soft, iridescent feathers in bright colors. The room was filled with plant life resembling mangroves. The "bird-ape" lay asleep on a pile of soft materials that looked like cotton or fluffy wads of wool. The floor was covered in desert sand. They moved on slowly, and Lennart marveled at the different habitats designed to replicate the home environments of each species.

Right next to that was another habitat, which looked empty at first glance. But upon closer inspection, Lennart spotted a slight, transparent creature, somewhat resembling a jellyfish. It had a vaguely human form but appeared fragile, with thin skin that allowed its glass-like skeleton to be seen through. Its organs looked like they were made of thick jelly, and you could see its heart beating through the translucent flesh. It was a bit unsettling. The creature's room was similar to Lennart's, and it sat at a desk, using an embedded tablet, apparently engrossed. It must have been highly intelligent. The room was filled with a faint bluish mist.

Lennart could never have imagined seeing such exotic life forms in his life. He was overwhelmed by the sight of these intelligent beings, each so unique. Together, they headed toward the elevators. Lennart had taken this same route in a panicked rush during his escape attempt, barely noticing his surroundings in his anxiety.

When they reached the elevators, they turned down another side corridor in the star-shaped layout of the hallways on that floor. It was a corridor full of countless expressions of life. He couldn't help but smile inwardly, thinking of Earth's humans who considered themselves the pinnacle of creation. They had no idea how richly populated the universe truly was. The beauty of the native inhabitants was remarkable. These peaceful beings seemed far more intelligent than humans in every way—technology, social understanding, creativity, and even physical strength. And, if Eugene's words were to be believed, they also surpassed humans in terms of life expectancy.

Suddenly, Lennart thought of Eugene, his late roommate. Thoughtfully, he murmured to himself, "Oh, Eugene, you had it all wrong all those years. If you had only eaten the fruit, you might have been home long ago. Then again, maybe Abron or anyone else had no interest in taking you by the hand and showing you this strange fruit's effect. May you rest in peace!"

As he thought of Abron, Abron rounded the corner carrying two fruit bowls, his long arms wrapping around one in each hand, making him look even broader than usual. He was surprised to see Lennart and Zafina in the corridor. After exchanging a few words with her, he turned his attention to Lennart. Then he said, "mi schuk do amam di ruck. Asam mi kudlahrah Ulam," followed by a sharp hissing sound.

Lennart finally understood what Abron had been trying to convey all along. The hissing meant "breathe," and the message was something like, "If you want to breathe in this atmosphere, you must eat the ULAM fruit." He let out a chuckle and nodded at the two of them.

Then he continued on his way. The two of them also began moving slowly. Though Lennart was supported, the gravity was beginning to wear him down, so they stopped every now and then to rest. Originally, Zafina wanted to walk him around the hallway a bit and even take him outside. But she realized that his muscles were too weak to manage such a walk. And because the effects of the fruit were still active, she couldn't take him back to his room just yet, or he'd start to hyperventilate from the high oxygen levels there. So they stopped by the elevators to rest for a moment. He leaned back against the wall, looking at her, wanting to ask the name of the planet they were on. He made a sphere with his hands, as if holding a large snowball, and pointed at the ground. She gave him a small smile and replied, "ALLCON." "Aha, Allcon!" he repeated. Then he made the same air-globe gesture, this time pointing at himself, and said slowly, "Earth." She nodded approvingly and responded, "Lennart, Eugen, Earth." "Wow, she's smart," he thought. He gathered his energy, and they slowly made their way back the way they had come.

As they passed by the transparent creature's habitat, it focused on Lennart as they walked by. The creature observed him intently, studying every movement, every step. Even inside the glass habitat, it followed them as they walked, until the back wall finally blocked its view. By this point, the effects of the oxygen-enriching fruit were beginning to fade. Lennart started gasping for air more frequently. Luckily, they were almost back to his room, where he could breathe normally. If it had taken any longer, he might have been in trouble. Altogether, he'd been in the hostile environment for about an hour. Zafina pulled on her breathing mask, guiding the now thoroughly exhausted Lennart through the airlock and back into his room. She helped him onto his cot, gently stroking his hair, and was about to leave when Lennart took her hand. He looked into her beautiful eyes and said, "Thank you, Zafina!" When he noticed that she didn't quite grasp his words, he took her hand between both of his and pressed it to his forehead, then kissed the back of her hand. He repeated softly, "Thank you, Zafina!" She was touched. She nodded slowly, smiled, and left.

Lennart felt so grateful that she had patiently and tirelessly guided him through this experience. Despite the effort of breathing and the increased gravity, he no longer felt like a prisoner. On the contrary, he was being given the freedom to move about in his surroundings. This was a great gift that gave him hope of one day returning home. Overjoyed but utterly exhausted, he fell into a contented sleep.

He slept for hours. Feeling refreshed and in a good mood, he got up, ate some delicious fruits, and danced to the whale song music. He then went to the bathroom and took a long shower under the waterfall. Back in his room, he scratched his now-long beard. The stubble was bothering him, and he began to wonder how he could shave. He remembered Eugen's pocketknife. When he went to the dresser to retrieve it, he was surprised to find that the knife, the pocket watch, and his phone were gone. Perhaps Abron or Zafina had taken them—maybe as a precaution or for safety reasons since he now had the freedom to move around in the habitat. After all, one could do quite a bit of damage with a knife. But something about it didn't quite make sense. He couldn't exactly harm anyone with a pocket watch or a phone. He decided to ask Abron or Zafina about it the next time he saw them. It was all very mysterious to him.

To shave properly, he didn't just need a knife; he'd also need something like shaving cream—something to soften the hair. He thought for a while and remembered the paring knife Zafina had brought with the fruit bowl. That might work to trim his beard. He looked over the remaining fruits. "Maybe I can mash up one of these to make something oily enough to soften the hair," he thought. He carefully tested the blade of the paring knife with his thumb to see if it was sharp enough. Satisfied, he figured it might work. He picked up a banana-like fruit and placed it in the mortar, using the pestle to crush it into a pulp. Then he added a bit of water from the carafe until he had a thick mixture. He poured the fruit cream into a glass bowl, took the knife, and happily returned to the bathroom. Under warm running water, he wet his beard, then applied the fruit mixture to his facial hair, massaging it into his cheeks, around his lips, and down his neck. Then he let it sit for a short while.

He carefully took the knife and scraped the blade across his cheek with short, jerky movements. "Hmm... something's happening," he muttered to himself.

About an hour and many cuts later, Lennart was clean-shaven. He washed the remaining fruit pulp from his face under the waterfall. The bleeding from the cuts stopped fairly quickly. His skin stung a little after the shave, but he was glad to have gotten rid of the annoying stubble.

He then walked around the room to take stock. He wanted to check if anything was missing from his personal belongings. His keys, his wallet—everything else was there. A little later, Abron entered the room, bringing him fresh fruit. This time, Lennart said enthusiastically, "Ahhh Ulam!" Abron laughed heartily. Then Lennart tapped him briefly and pointed to the pile of his things on the dresser. He shrugged and turned his palms upward, signaling to Abron that he had no idea where his missing items had gone. Abron stared intently at the dresser, and after a few seconds, he seemed to understand that quite a bit was missing. He muttered something unintelligible and hurried out of the room.

A short while later, Abron returned with two other male planet inhabitants, bursting into Lennart's room. He explained something to them, pointing at the dresser. The two of them almost synchronously pulled out a device that resembled a tablet. Then, they quickly left the room again.

Lennart understood that Abron couldn't have been involved in the disappearance of his things. He had been visibly upset when he realized the loss. So upset, in fact, that he'd probably alerted two of his security officers. "I get that you can hurt someone with a knife, but who needs an old, stopped clock? And what's someone supposed to do with my dead phone?" Lennart wondered, still amazed by Abron's reaction and that of his two helpers. He was even more surprised when he looked through his glass window and saw them heading into his neighbor's habitat, clearly searching everything. When they found nothing, they went straight to the entrance of the next transparent being's dwelling, disappearing from view.

Since his walk with Zafina, Lennart had been feeling more motivated and wanted to further optimize his physical fitness to improve his endurance under gravity. He wanted to be strong enough to find the park again. So, he resumed his workout routine and did his three strength exercises, pushing himself until his muscles ached. After a short rest, he pushed himself even harder. He doubled the length of his workout. Ultimately, he wanted to be fit enough to get back home as quickly as possible. Completely exhausted, he went to the bathroom and showered under the waterfall until he felt fresh again.

After his shower, he ran his hand over his face and was surprised to find that the cuts he had gotten while shaving had completely healed. It must have been some advanced technology that sped up the healing process dramatically. He remembered arriving injured, with bruises, bumps, and scratches, and after waking up, being fully recovered. These highly developed beings must have access to technologies that not only accelerated healing but also prevented aging. Normally, Lennart wasn't athletic at all. He recalled the times when he would immediately get sore muscles after any kind of physical exercise, and it would usually last for several days. But here, everything was different.

Satisfied, he put on his garment after the shower and returned to his living space. He sat down at the desk, set the fruit bowl in front of him, picked some delicious fruit, and ate them leisurely. While eating, he thought about how he could get back home. Now, with the help of the Ulam fruit, he was able to move freely outside. One big hurdle had been overcome. Now, the challenge was to find the place where he had stranded without drawing too much attention. He figured that the best way to do this would be to blend in with the inhabitants of this planet. He already had a garment like theirs. Then he remembered how Zafina had made the paste and how it had the same color as the skin of the male beings. All he needed now was to figure out how to get the ornaments on his face.

Lennart wasn't particularly skilled at makeup. He pondered for a while until he remembered his recent purchase. He went to the dresser, grabbed the cheese, whole grain bread, and water bottle. He sat back down at the desk with these three items and tossed them into the glass bowl. The cheese was already moldy and smelled bad. The whole grain bread was covered in mold as well. "Well, I don't need to eat these anymore," he thought and poured enough water from the bottle over the mixture. He let the ingredients soak for a bit. From time to time, he stirred the mixture with his hands until it reached a consistency similar to dough. The room's fountain stood next to the desk, and he occasionally washed his hands there. Then he did exactly what Zafina had done. He took some starfruit and the remaining Ulam fruit and placed them in the mortar, pouring water from the jug until a purple paste formed. He grabbed the bowl with his makeshift modeling clay and the mortar with the dyed paste. Then, he went back to the bathroom.

There, he removed his garment and spread the paste over his arms, hands, face, legs, and feet. He waited until the paste dried on him. He looked at his arms and was quite pleased with the result. The color now resembled that of the male planet inhabitants. Next, he dipped his fingertips into the glass bowl, kneaded a ball of paste, and rubbed the bread-and-cheese mixture between his palms. Pressing harder, a thin, sticky, long roll formed. He shaped it in his hands until it took on an S-shape. He placed it across his forehead. The paste was very sticky and adhered well to his face. He repeated this process three more times, covering his cheeks and the chin just below his lip with the self-made ornaments. Finally, he waited until the ornaments on his face hardened slightly, then took a bit of the dyed paste from the mortar and gently stroked it over the claywork to match the purple color of the male All-coner inhabitants.

Lennart was pretty sure it was far from perfect, but it would do for now to let him move around outside without attracting too much attention. Then he took the glass bowl and the mortar back to his living room. There, he rinsed both in the room's fountain and prepared the same fruit mixture with starfruit and Ulam fruits again. This time, though, he made it to drink so he could breathe better in the thin atmosphere. His plan was to find the place outside that would allow him to get back home. So he quickly drank down the paste he'd prepared following Zafina's recipe. He walked slowly toward the decompression chamber and waited impatiently for his blood to fill with oxygen. Soon enough, that familiar tingling sensation began to spread through his whole body. His fists started to clench up again, but he didn't wait until they were fully cramped. To get out, he'd need to lay his hand flat on the monitor. So he stood with his hand outstretched, ready to press the monitor at the perfect moment. Just before his fists tightened again, he timed it perfectly, and it worked like a charm.

And so Lennart, dressed like a local and feeling both determined and a bit wistful, set off toward the elevators as quickly as he could. Amazingly, there were hardly any visitors in the halls who might have noticed him. When he reached the ground floor, he headed straight to the glass front doors and left the building. He was proud of himself for having figured out a way around the toughest obstacles. Outside, no one seemed to pay much attention to him. First, he took a long loop around the building to orient himself better, keeping an eye out for the skyscraper topped with a statue of a hero striking a victorious pose over the city. On the far side of the habitat building, he finally spotted the building he'd been looking for in the distance. Lennart felt as excited as a kid. Cautiously and slowly, he started walking toward the skyscraper. But he soon realized it was simply too far to reach on foot with the dose of Ulam fruit he'd taken. His knees were already shaking from the effort. So, making a sensible decision for once, he turned back toward the habitat. For him, though, it still felt like a victory march because he now knew where his goal was.

Back in the habitat, he took the elevator up. By then, he was so exhausted he had to brace himself against the walls with each step. Finally, he stopped at his door and waited patiently for the fruit's effects to wear off. Once again, he timed the moment perfectly, stepping into the small decompression chamber, and with the last of his strength, made his way into his quarters. Back in his room, he could breathe normally again. The whole outing had been so strenuous and had drained so much of his energy that he went straight for the water jug, downing half a liter in one go. Just as he was heading toward his lounge chair to rest from the trip, the door opened, and Zafina entered the room.

For a moment, she just stared at him, completely dumbfounded. Then she suddenly burst out laughing so hard that Lennart felt a little alarmed. Zafina was practically doubled over, clutching her stomach as she laughed. Lennart, looking like a male planet inhabitant, must have been a hilarious sight. Pink tears streamed down her cheeks as she gasped and squealed with laughter. She dashed out of the room for a moment. Lennart stood there, feeling slightly embarrassed, not moving an inch. Through the glass, he saw Zafina still laughing, slapping her thigh, and then waving someone over. Abron hurried over and took one look at Lennart before bursting out laughing as well. Both of them entered his room, and Abron pulled a small, flat device from his suit, holding it in Lennart's direction. There was a quick flash, and then the device projected a holographic image of Lennart in 3D between the three of them.

It took several minutes for them to finally stop laughing. Lennart chuckled a bit too, seeing himself like that in 3D. He really did look a bit ridiculous.

But there was one thing he didn't know and would only discover later, after they had left, when he tried to wash off the dye. It was like henna—it wouldn't come off at all. As he scrubbed his ornaments under the shower, revealing the light skin underneath, his dyed body parts stayed stubbornly purple. He'd been quite generous with the dye on his face. He scrubbed and washed and rinsed, but nothing helped. Lennart cursed his usual mantra: "Damn, damn it all—damn, damn it all!" Apparently, both Zafina and Abron had known that the dye was permanent. Now, he could only hope that the pigments wouldn't take too long to fade. From the moment he was back in his room after showering, there were often cheerful visitors at his window, laughing good-naturedly at the sight.

6. People's Representative

Time was running out for Felix. If he wasn't released soon, he'd lose his job. He hoped that his lawyer's intervention had worked and that any misunderstandings had been cleared up. He also hoped that Nicole would confirm his alibi. Now, everything was on the line. Felix was brought before the magistrate. He was assigned a seat, and the charges against him were read out. He was questioned once again. "Felix Schulte, do you have anything to do with the disappearance of your acquaintance, Lennart Neumann?" Felix replied, "Absolutely not! Quite the opposite. I was the one who reported Lennart missing because I was worried about my friend. I never intended to hide or destroy evidence, as accused. I only wanted to help, albeit somewhat naively. I wanted to be there to support the police in any way I could. I was in a café with two friends when Lennart disappeared. I've provided all the evidence I have to the police. Please believe me—I am completely innocent."

Then there was silence. The judge looked carefully over his notes. Felix's statement, Nicole's testimony, and his lawyer's excellent work had saved him at the last moment. However, he was still ordered to stay out of the investigation, except if requested, and only to act as instructed. Then came the acquittal. Felix felt a thousand kilos lift off his shoulders. But it would still be hours before he was actually released, as the wheels of justice turn slowly. The bureaucratic process—certificates, file entries, computer records—took hours before he could finally taste freedom.

Finally, Felix received his personal belongings that had been taken from him, along with a document notifying him when he could retrieve his computer. After his release, his father picked him up and took him straight home. Felix decided that after this ordeal and the shock it had caused him, he would rest at home for a few days before dealing with his computer. He was so relieved to be free again. Once home, he turned on his phone to check for any missed calls or messages. Except for some spam emails, no one had noticed he was gone. He realized that while Nicole had provided her statement when asked by the police, she otherwise hadn't shown much interest in him. He decided to be grateful for her truthful statement, but to leave her as a distant acquaintance. He wouldn't be reaching out to her.

While in custody, he had thought of Lennart constantly. He missed him, and it was only now that he fully realized it. Among all the people he knew, there was only one true friend. He felt a deep sadness. It had already been two more days without any sign of life from Lennart, and Felix's hopes for his survival were fading fast. It had been made clear to him that he needed to stay out of the search for Lennart. He rested, went grocery shopping, cooked himself a meal, and prepared to get back to his life the next day. This meant going to work, visiting his parents, and focusing on daily routines—anything to distract himself from the fact that he was powerless to help Lennart. He thought of Lennart's parents too. Those poor people, they must be going through hell. Not knowing if their son was alive, if he'd ever be found—this was surely the worst thing they'd ever had to endure. Felix felt tremendous sympathy.

The next day, when Lennart woke up, he was stunned. As he got up from his cot and looked through the window, he saw a gathering of local inhabitants standing directly in front of his room. He went closer to the glass to see why he was attracting so much attention. He glanced down at himself. His skin was still purple, but that probably wasn't the reason. The crowd arranged themselves in a semicircle around his habitat as if on cue. Then a very large, powerful-looking native stepped forward. Unlike the others, he wore a silver robe. He was even more imposing than Abron. He approached the glass, and as he did so, everyone around him bowed. Lennart began to feel scared. But since everyone else was doing it, he also gave a respectful bow. When he stood back up, his muscles were tense with fear. He had no idea what this was all about.

Facing Lennart was none other than the ruler of this planet, who had come in person to honor him. This ruler reminded Lennart of the statue in a victorious pose on top of the high building he had often looked for. He wondered if he was about to be judged. To his surprise, the ruler bowed back to him in a respectful greeting, then laughed, raising his hand. Lennart swallowed hard. As the ruler lowered his hand again, there was a burst of flashing lights. Apparently, the locals were eagerly photographing this significant moment. The ruler then turned his back to the window and addressed the crowd. He gestured with his strong, muscular arms while the flashing lights from their devices continued. Lennart's heart was pounding in his chest. After several minutes, the crowd dispersed. The proud leader moved on, followed by his followers. Once the crowd cleared, only one person remained—Abron. As usual, he had a bowl of fruit with him.

When everyone else had left, Abron approached Lennart's room, put on his breathing mask, and entered the decompression chamber. A moment later, he stepped inside with a beaming smile. He set the fruit bowl down, then bowed respectfully before Lennart, just as he had when they first met. Lennart returned the gesture with a polite bow, although he still didn't fully understand why all this fuss was being made over him. Abron then swung his long arm in a grand circle, gesturing toward where the ruler had been standing. "Lemar," Abron said in his deep voice. Lennart repeated, "Aha, King Lemar," giving a slow, respectful Japanese-style bow to show he understood that Lemar was an important, respected figure. Abron nodded in satisfaction, smiling at Lennart as he repeated once again, "Aha, King Lemar!" Then he flexed his arm, showing off a powerful bicep to indicate that this Lemar must be incredibly strong.

Lennart nodded in agreement a few times. This guy was without a doubt a giant. Abron was about to leave, but Lennart pointed at his dresser again to remind him of his missing items. Abron's first search had obviously led to nothing. Both of them froze in place when they noticed that his wallet and car keys had also disappeared. Alarmed, Abron dashed out and called his assistants again. Lennart scratched his head, puzzled. He couldn't figure out who or what could've quietly sneaked into his room while he was asleep and gradually swiped his belongings. What could anyone on Allcon possibly want with these items? Most likely, even his empty shopping bag, which he'd used to help him breathe, had been taken in this way. It dawned on Lennart that none of the doors were locked; any being capable of doing so could have entered at any time. He decided to continue his training program, as exercising helped him in two ways: he could stay outside longer in the high gravity, and after these sneaky thefts, he'd be more prepared to defend himself if he ever encountered the thief. Energized, he jumped back into his three exercises, and each time, the push-ups—which had once been so exhausting—became easier. He trained until he was utterly spent, then stepped into the refreshing waterfall shower. He looked at his still-violet skin, rubbing and scrubbing his arms, but the color wouldn't wash off. Quietly, he mumbled his little "damn it" mantra.

After his shower, dressed again, he entered his room, grabbed the choicest fruits from the basket, and dug in—he was starving after his workout. Sitting at his desk, he decided to try to figure out the tablet attached there. He swiped his finger left to right, then top to bottom. The symbols and unfamiliar characters shifted with each swipe. Sometimes the music got louder, sometimes quieter. At one point, it stopped completely, only to start up again. He kept going until he recognized a pattern and could at least control the music. In the end, he left the settings as they were; he found the music relaxing and enjoyable. After a while, he felt like going outside again. He set out some Ulam and starfruit, considering whether to wait for Zafina or head out on his own.

Naturally, he felt safer and better with her by his side, but he didn't know when, or even if, she'd stop by again. Somehow, he missed her—her sparkling green eyes, her beautiful face. "These beings are so intelligent," he thought. "Compared to them, maybe I'm no smarter than a dog next to a human." That thought saddened him, and at the same time, he felt a strong longing for home. He missed Felix terribly and thought of his poor parents, who were probably sick with worry by now, since he hadn't contacted them in days. He grew even sadder when he thought of Eugen, who had spent his whole life here. What if he didn't manage to return either?

Lost in thought, he slammed his fist on the tabletop. "No, no, no, that can't be! I have to make it back somehow, whatever it takes. I have to get back home!" Lennart felt himself sinking into a mild depression, overwhelmed by the daunting task of getting back safely. The gravity, the limited breathing, the distance to the tower—he had no idea what he'd even do once he got there to find his way back to where he'd come from. The more he thought about it, the sadder he became. Finally, he couldn't hold back the tears, quietly sobbing to himself.

After a moment, he pulled himself together, gathering his strength. He decided he would find the shortest path home. He took the mortar, the water jug, and the fruit and made a new batch of Ulam pulp. This time he added an extra fruit of each kind, filling the glass bowl to the brim. There was even some left in the mortar. Then he placed the bowl and mortar next to his bed on the dresser, planning to rest a bit before tackling the whole serving. As he lay down, he drifted off to sleep, only to wake up a short while later to a noise. Abron was in his room again, looking at the dresser and shaking his head. Lennart's things were still missing.

"The crime rate on Allcon must be really low," Lennart thought. "Higher beings obviously have no need to take possessions that belong to others. Abron probably isn't much of a detective; he likely can't even imagine what it's like to think like a thief." Lennart decided he'd have to handle this himself for now. Abron waved him goodbye and left the room. Lennart began to ponder. He suddenly remembered that curious, transparent creature that had watched him so intently when he'd been strolling down the hall with Zafina.

This creature was behaving very suspiciously, and with its transparent appearance, it could easily slip through the hallways almost unnoticed. Apart from his and Eugen's clothing and the symbolic key to freedom that still hung around his neck, everything else had been taken from him. He paused for a moment and decided that since Zafina hadn't shown up, he'd explore the building on his own. Taking the glass bowl, he drank the Ulam smoothie in one gulp, carefully setting the bowl back on the dresser. Then he took the mortar and emptied it as well. Waiting for the effect to kick in, he walked to the center of the room and rinsed the empty containers under the small fountain. Finally, he sat back down on his bed until he felt the familiar tingling spreading through his body.

Almost out of habit, he got up and went to the door, entering the airlock chamber. Timing it perfectly to avoid any muscle cramps, he pressed his hand flat on the panel to open the door and headed straight down the corridor without wasting a moment, directly toward the habitat of the transparent creature. He stopped outside its chamber and observed. "Ugh, how weird and creepy it is to see into the body through the skin," Lennart thought, as he watched the creature sitting crosslegged, meditating with its eyes closed. He could see the dark brown blood circulating, the heartbeat, and the lungs slowly expanding and contracting with each breath. He inspected it intently, scrutinizing every movement, while also looking over the room from the outside. Muttering to himself, he thought, "My things have to be hidden here somewhere! If I were hiding something, where would I put it?" The room itself was almost identical to Lennart's, so he could only think of three potential hiding places: under the bed, scattered among the exotic plants, or somewhere in the waterfall bath. He examined the bed for any unusual bulges but found nothing. He paced along the glass wall, trying to see between the plants from every possible angle. Still nothing.

How he'd love to go in there and pay that scrawny creature a little visit. He was sure he'd find his belongings hidden between the smooth, rounded stones in that little bathroom. As Lennart stood there, perplexed, a few Allcon inhabitants passed by at irregular intervals. Since Lemar's visit, each resident now made a polite bow as they passed him. Lennart always returned the gesture, although he wasn't sure of its exact significance; staying on good terms with the Allconians seemed wise enough. After the last person bowed and moved on, he turned back to the glass, only to jump several times in fright. The transparent creature had noticed him and was now right in front of his face, separated only by the glass pane. Huge pitch-black eyes stared back at him. "Holy crap!" Lennart exclaimed, jumping back instinctively. Under his breath, he muttered, "Good grief, you scared the heck out of me!" His heart pounded furiously, and it took him a while to calm down. He would have liked to continue observing the strange creature discreetly, but at first glance, nothing indicated that this scrawny being, living in a bluish mist, could even leave its habitat. He began to doubt whether this creature was the thief and decided to move on, considering other possible culprits.

Lennart pondered how to approach his investigation systematically to make the best use of the limited time he had. The best plan was to start from the farthest area and gradually work his way back toward his own habitat. That way, if the effect of the fruit began to fade, he wouldn't be far from his room and could return to breathe normally if needed. So he headed straight to the elevator and went up to the highest level, the fourteenth floor. Once there, he realized that the only thing around him was a single ring-shaped habitat. Looking up through the round, glass dome of the building, he saw the stunning orange sky. There it was again—the huge, beautiful, turquoise-blue moon. The smaller silver moon wasn't visible in the sky. He stood there, feeling moved, taking in the breathtaking view. Thin, line-shaped clouds drifted slowly above him in parallel patterns.

Lennart was so struck by the overwhelming beauty of this world that two tears rolled slowly down his cheeks. Then he walked around the ring-shaped habitat, which was dark inside and devoid of any furniture. The only things he could see were a few small points of light, shimmering faintly blue in the darkness, like tiny fireflies floating weightlessly in the air. Their movements were rhythmic but followed no specific order. These slow, rhythmic motions filled Lennart with an inner peace he had never known before. Everything felt so harmonious. It was, in a way, spiritual. It felt as if he had finally arrived somewhere. The burning need to return home was gone. A deep sense of contentment spread within him. It was as if the next moment didn't matter and all that counted was the present.

Lennart sat down on the floor and watched the gently moving points of light as if hypnotized. He felt so rich. Rich with life energy—an abundance of life energy. Then he closed his eyes and fully absorbed this moment of being in the now. He felt so well that he wished this moment would never end. A familiar warmth filled his heart, and the longer he sat there, the stronger this feeling grew. It was an intimate emotion, though he felt connected to the entire world. Somehow, it felt paradoxical, but in his state, it made complete sense. His inner dialogue had quieted, and he was fully alert. Every second was imbued with deep awareness. He was completely aware of himself.

Whereas earlier he had shed only two tears, now they flowed freely. He cried hard but smiled through the tears. Then, slowly, thoughts began to return. A clear, inner voice spoke to him. He allowed the thoughts to come. The strange part was that, unlike his usual thoughts, which he assumed came directly from him, this time he could sit beside them, as if observing his own thinking. It was as if he were sitting next to himself, watching his own thoughts unfold from a distance.

7. Dialogue

Lennart slowly opened his eyes. A deep peace flowed through his entire body. In the habitat, the light particles had gathered together, forming a shape. Like a school of fish, each particle joined to create a larger figure. They shaped themselves into a seated figure on the ground, mirroring Lennart as he sat there in spiritual ecstasy. The shape appeared right in front of him. The inner voice he had heard grew clearer: "Greetings, child of Earth. I welcome you, Lennart. You have come here from afar, and though it was unintentional, I am pleased by your visit. This is the first time a human has connected with me in thought."

Lennart's heartbeat slowed, keeping a steady rhythm as he replied in his mind, "Hello, beautiful being. If you are responsible for the state I'm in, then I want to thank you from the bottom of my heart. My journey here to Allcon was a rare coincidence. At first, my experiences on this planet were a shock, but I've had the honor of meeting beings I never could have dreamed of. And now you. I thank you for the grace of elevating me spiritually. What kind of being are you? How can you know my language and my name?"

The answers to Lennart's questions came to him immediately, as though placed directly into his awareness: "I am of an ancient race that lives scattered across the universe. We are called the Todax. We are nearly as old as the universe itself. Our mission is to support life's evolution in every star system. There is even one of my kind residing in your own solar system. Humanity, however, is still in the early stages of development, and only a very few of you have any potential for higher evolution. But your time will come. You can understand me because you have opened yourself to this. You hear my soundless sound because your heart is in the right place. You understand me because you accept the timeless now. I know your name and your language because you allowed me to connect with you. In such a connection, words become unnecessary, as we understand each other universally. By allowing me to be a guest within you, I know your name."

Lennart remained still, seated on the ground, yet a torrent of new questions arose within him: "I have so many questions. If one of your kind also lives in Earth's solar system, has it already made contact with humans? Will we, as humans, manage to evolve to the same level as the beings here on Allcon? Where is Allcon in relation to Earth? Are we far from home?"

Once again, the answers came to him, filling his mind. "The Todax are beings unbound by place. We exist as small elemental particles, so tiny that we can permeate any material. I, too, am not confined to this location but choose to be here. We are always connected and communicate across vast distances. We radiate an unending peace, and advanced beings can effortlessly perceive our messages. A few humans, though very few, have also connected with this universal peace. Currently, humanity is still affected by selfishness. But you are only at the beginning of your journey. Thankfully, growth is inevitable. You will develop and expand your consciousness. Allcon is about 40 light-years from Earth. From your perspective, we are in the constellation of Aquarius. Humans call this star system Trappist. For now, your questions have been answered. You must return, as the effects of the Ulam fruit will soon fade. We should continue our dialogue another time. Lastly, know this—you are more than you think you are."

Lennart gave a brief nod to the being of light and spoke one last time, "Thank you from the depths of my heart for this conversation. I am so grateful to have met you, and I look forward to meeting again." He rose and walked toward the elevator. The second voice within him fell silent.

He descended to the second floor and stepped out. His breathing grew labored. He estimated that he'd spent a good two or three hours in the low-oxygen environment. He hurried to the decompression chamber, feeling the strain in his lungs. Just in time, he reached his room. "Wow, what an experience," he marveled at the emotional state the light being had given him. Lennart savored every moment, wondering if the great spiritual masters of Earth had also felt this way when they spoke of blissful peace. As he lay back on his bed, he chuckled softly to himself. His skin was still purple.

He remembered how much Zafina had laughed at his odd appearance. The dialogue with the telepathic being still echoed within him, especially that final sentence: that he was more than he thought. What could that have meant? The calming music in his room and the deeply peaceful state he felt began to fill Lennart with renewed hope of returning home. Forty light-years away. At least now he had some kind of measurement he could start to make sense of. And knowing he was still in the Milky Way—his home galaxy—made the insane distance somehow a bit more comprehensible. Lennart didn't really know what the Aquarius constellation looked like. Even if he were looking up at the night sky from Earth, he wouldn't have been able to identify it; he simply didn't know enough about astronomy. He also realized he had never heard of the Trappist solar system before.

Gradually, a sense of normalcy returned to Lennart. He thought for a while about his current situation. He had a lot of free time, but nothing with which to fill it in a meaningful way. He longed for a few basic things, wishing he could somehow record what he was experiencing. A pen, a camera, some paper—anything would do. Unfortunately, his phone was gone, and even if he had it, the battery was dead. How fantastic it would have been if he could return to Earth with photos or videos. Photos of the inhabitants of this amazing planet, the beings living in these habitats, the gigantic, beautifully turquoise moon. He would also have loved to jot down notes about fragments of conversation he'd overheard from the Allcon residents. And of course, the thoughts he had shared with the telepathic being. He wished he could have documented the exotic plants and fruits he ate each day.

Then he remembered that it would soon be time for another shave. Surely it would be a hundred times easier with a sharp blade rather than with the vegetable peeler he'd been using. Some shaving cream would make the whole process so much simpler. Without it, shaving was painfully slow. He thought that when Zafina came by next, he could go with her to the top floor to communicate with the telepathic life form and explain what he really needed. Hopefully, Zafina and the Todax would agree to help. It would certainly make things easier if he could get his requests across clearly. If the being could communicate mentally with Lennart, then it could certainly pass on his thoughts to Zafina.

He realized then that he hadn't seen her in a while. Surely she had her own life and other things to do besides looking after him. If that was the case, maybe Abron could help out instead, though he'd definitely prefer Zafina. She simply had more patience with him. Without her, he'd still be sitting cluelessly in his room, much like poor Eugen had been.

Sticking to his routine, Lennart got ready to do his exercises. This time, he felt hardly weakened by his outing; admittedly, he hadn't moved around much but had mostly just been sitting in the upper floor. Just as he was about to get up, he noticed Abron through his window, darting around the neighboring habitats with baskets of fruit. As Abron passed by his room, Lennart tapped quickly on the window to catch his attention. Abron looked over, and Lennart gestured for him to come into his room.

He wanted to ask if there had been any progress in finding his belongings. He also wanted to ask about Zafina. So there he was, with Abron standing in front of him in his protective suit and breathing mask. Lennart bowed politely to greet Abron in a traditional way. Abron bowed back almost at the same time and gave Lennart a questioning look, trying to figure out why he had been invited in. Lennart gestured with an outstretched hand toward his metal dresser, hoping to ask if his things had shown up by now. "Ngo," Abron replied in a deep voice, shaking his head. This was clearly a "no." Apparently, there was still no sign of the missing items.

Next, Lennart pointed to his chin, where stubble was starting to grow back, and he ran his hand over his scratchy beard. Trying to mime shaving wasn't easy, especially since the Allcon inhabitants didn't grow facial hair. He rubbed his chin with his fingernails, trying to suggest that he'd like to scrape the stubble off. Abron examined Lennart's beard growth closely but just shrugged; he clearly didn't understand. "Ah, never mind!" Lennart waved it off. Then, he raised one finger and wiggled his fingers as if playing an invisible piano, hoping to mimic the floating particles of the telepathic creature, and then pointed upwards again. "Granted," he thought, "it does take a fair bit of imagination to interpret this." Unfortunately, Abron didn't understand this either and shrugged once more.

Lennart persisted. "Zafina, where's Zafina?" he asked eagerly. In response, he received a long string of completely unintelligible words. Lennart shrugged this time; he didn't understand a thing. He knew it wouldn't do much good to mime out his request for pen and paper, either. "The Allconers probably keep everything digitally and don't use paper at all," Lennart mused. Finally, they waved goodbye to each other, and Abron left Lennart's room. Feeling a bit dejected by the failed conversation, Lennart went to his desk, turned up the soothing music, and set to his workout. Training to exhaustion, he hoped to build more muscle.

The exercises felt easier every day, so he just kept going until he couldn't anymore. When he finally finished, muscles trembling and exhausted, he ended his routine with a relaxing shower under the waterfall. Showering was when his best ideas came to him. He thought about how he could improvise a writing tool and paper from the things and materials lying around. "I could make a colored ink just like I used to dye my skin, just mix it myself! And for paper, I'll see if there's anything useful in my room." Maybe he could dry some plant leaves or cut up Eugen's clothes into small, even pieces.

Lost in thought, he went over to his lounge chair after the shower, filled up on exotic fruit, and lay down to relax. He set aside the Ulam fruits, realizing that he had too few of them for all he wanted to do. He'd need to ration them carefully if he was to have enough for trips outside and to extract pigment for drawing. He thought he could gradually sketch the inhabitants and other creatures he met, adding descriptions to each drawing. He also wanted to keep a journal and record his experiences day by day. Finally, he thought he'd start learning the Allconers' language and put together a vocabulary list.

He listened to the music a bit longer, trying to keep hold of the peaceful feeling. Pleased with his ideas, he closed his eyes and soon drifted into a deep sleep.

Felix was at work when he received an email from his supervisor. He was more than a little surprised when he saw the subject line: "Invitation to an Employee Meeting." His supervisor sat just one door away, yet here he was, reaching out formally. "This can't be a good sign," Felix muttered to himself. He had already noticed a change in how his colleagues were treating him. The meeting was scheduled for that afternoon. It was possible this had something to do with Lennart's disappearance. After all, the police had come to question people at work. "Not good at all!" he realized. His boss was always so strict, and now with the police involved, it really didn't look good for him. Ever since then, his colleagues had been distant. At first, he'd assumed they were just busy and didn't have time for small talk. He thought to himself, "I'm sure I can answer all their questions, and everything will smooth over. After all, I have nothing to hide. When a friend goes missing and you turn to the police for help, the boss should be able to understand, right?"

He then briefly ran through all the possibilities, wondering if by chance he'd made a mistake at work that he hadn't noticed. He checked his recent activities on his computer and quickly reviewed the printed documents on his desk. "Everything looks fine here! It can't be that," he concluded. So, as far as work went, everything was in order. Then it could only be about his brief time in police custody. Until the scheduled meeting, Felix kept working as usual, trying to cover up his inner unease with his routine tasks.

When it was time for the meeting, he knocked on his boss's door. His boss invited him in and kindly offered him a seat across from him. Then he got right to the point, asking, "Hey Felix, how are you doing?" Felix replied, "Considering the circumstances, I'm a bit shaken. My best friend has vanished without a trace. When I tried to ask the police for help, there was a huge misunderstanding. I was even wrongfully arrested and barely made it back to work on time. There's no sugarcoating it—I'm depressed." With a serious expression, his boss continued, "That's exactly what I wanted to talk to you about today. The mood in the office has taken a big hit because of the police visit and all the uncomfortable questions. That's already a problem. But what's really bad is that, when the police were here asking uncomfortable questions about you, one of our most important clients happened to be in the building and decided to walk away from us because of it. I've worked hard for years to build up a positive image for this company. Now we have a problem: colleagues are whispering, and clients are backing out. I understand that you're dealing with a difficult situation personally, but we can't overlook the impact it's having here. So I'm suggesting we end our collaboration. The best way forward is if we agree on a mutual termination. We'll set it for the end of the month, and until then, you'll be on leave to take care of your personal matters. Of course, you'll receive a fair severance package."

Felix was stunned and asked, with a shaky voice, "Do you really think this is necessary? Can't we bring things back on track?" His boss shook his head and concluded, "Believe me, this wasn't an easy decision. Ultimately, it's not about you personally. It's more a matter of unfortunate circumstances." Felix gave in and eventually agreed to the termination. He saw little point in fighting for a job where no one wanted him around anymore. And so he left his supervisor's office. He packed his personal belongings with a heavy heart, cleaned up his desk, and said goodbye to each of his colleagues individually. Felix completed all the paperwork at HR and then drove home in a sad daze.

On the way home, he called his parents to discuss what had happened. His father suggested he get a lawyer to fight for his rights. His mother, on the other hand, advised him to think things over, register as unemployed for now, focus on taking care of himself, and then look for a new job. She said it was sad how people get treated in the workplace, but it wasn't the end of the world, and with his skills, he would surely find a good position again soon.

8. Todax

In the dead of night, Lennart was abruptly jolted out of his peaceful sleep by a sharp tugging at his neck. As he opened his eyes, he saw a huge silhouette looming over him. Someone was trying to slip the key to freedom—left to him by Eugen—off his neck while he slept. Terrified, Lennart began flailing his arms wildly, shouting loudly for help. He fought with all his might, trying to keep the intruder at bay, pushing him away with his outstretched hands. Realizing Lennart's resistance and cries for help, the nighttime thief decided to abandon his mission and tried to flee. Lennart chased him to the door and managed to grab him by the hair, ripping off something soft from his skin. But in one swift motion, the thief struck Lennart with such force that he was knocked out in an instant. The powerful figure vanished, and Lennart collapsed to the floor. Everything went still and dark.

When Lennart came to, his room was brightly lit. Abron was bent over him with a worried expression, gently dabbing Lennart's forehead with a cool compress. Beside him stood his two loyal security guards, talking loudly to Abron in their native language. Frantically, Lennart felt for the key around his neck, checking to see if it was still there. Yes, the key was still in place. He felt faint with relief, but the pain made him cry out. As he touched his neck, a few colorful, soft feathers slipped from his hand and drifted slowly to the floor. Lennart's logical thinking was clouded, but Abron immediately understood—it had to be the feathered, humanoid bird-creature, the being who lived practically right across from Lennart. Abron gave instructions to his security team, pointing with an outstretched hand at the habitat across the hall from Lennart's.

The bio-monitors on the walls of Lennart's room were blinking in all sorts of colors, repeatedly showing images of his head and beeping softly in alarm. He had a serious injury to his head, a bleeding wound that throbbed painfully. Lennart clutched his head in agony, twisting from side to side, his face contorted in pain, on the verge of collapse. Abron pulled a small, handheld device from his suit and held it a few centimeters from Lennart's wound. The pain subsided, and Lennart quickly drifted off to sleep, sedated by Abron's intervention. No wonder—Abron had effectively put him to sleep. At that moment, two more staff members entered the room, both medical professionals. They brought a few suitcase-sized devices and began tending to Lennart. Abron was asked to leave the room, so he stood outside, waiting as the medics dealt with the emergency. Then he briefly checked in with his security team to see how they were managing with the feathered orangutan-like creature.

The intruder lay stunned on the sandy floor while the two Allconian security officers searched the room for stolen items. From the soft pile of wool that served as the creature's bed, they pulled out a variety of objects. This thieving, unruly creature had amassed a whole collection of stolen goods over time. Various items emerged—many glittering or reflecting light, some metallic, others electronic. Much of the stash didn't just belong to Lennart but had been taken from other beings as well; it was simply that some hadn't noticed, or didn't care.

After the security team had thoroughly searched the thief's quarters, Abron reprogrammed the room's exit mechanism to open only with a special code—a safety measure to ensure that no one else would be injured, and no more items could be stolen. The security officers and Abron stood at the observation window to Lennart's room, watching the medics busily tend to him. On Earth, Lennart would not have survived, and even here on Allcon, his situation was still critical. He was suffering from severe internal brain hemorrhaging. Medical technology on this planet was highly advanced, but the real question was, to what extent had his brain been damaged?

The Allconians scanned all parts of Lennart's body and monitored his functions. Then they compared any deviations from the baseline against his recorded values. In Lennart's case, the discrepancies were so significant that they injected countless microscopic robots into his wound to restore his body to its programmed state. It took over five hours before all the readings returned to normal. But even after the procedure, they kept Lennart in a sedated state to spare him as much pain as possible. An entire day passed before Lennart regained consciousness. When he awoke, Zafina was sitting by his bedside, holding his hand. Lennart had a pounding headache but was grateful to see her. He had fragmentary memories of the night he was attacked, but they were faint. He knew that something unexpected had happened, but that was all. His memory was foggy.

As he tried to sit up, a wave of dizziness washed over him, and he fell back onto the bed, clutching his throbbing head. Zafina whispered something to him, but of course, he couldn't understand a word.

When he awoke, Zafina was sitting by his bedside, holding his hand. Lennart had a pounding headache, but seeing her brought him relief. His memories of the night he was attacked were fragmented—fleeting images and sensations, barely tangible. He knew something unexpected had happened, but the details were missing. His memory had been compromised.

As he tried to sit up, his head throbbed so intensely that he fell back onto the bed. Zafina whispered something to him, but of course, he couldn't understand a word. She continued to gently stroke his hand. He wanted desperately to tell her something, but despite his best efforts, the words simply wouldn't come. Frustration bubbled up, and he grew agitated. It was a dangerous reaction—his heart began to race, sending more blood coursing through his veins. This strain triggered a sudden collapse, and Lennart lost consciousness.

The medical monitors around him blared in alarm. Zafina quickly called for the medics, who rushed in, assessed him, and induced a controlled artificial sleep to stabilize him. The healing process had been only partially successful. The medics asked Zafina to leave the room, explaining that they needed to proceed with another urgent round of treatment; otherwise, Lennart wouldn't survive.

Tears, a soft rosy hue unique to her species, streamed down Zafina's cheeks as she stepped aside. She and Abron had been taking turns staying by Lennart's side, ensuring he was never alone. This time, however, the treatment took far longer than before. Abron had done his best, but the gravity of the situation weighed heavily on him. He felt responsible, regretting that he had taken the initial incident too lightly.

Abron's guilt was compounded by his growing affection for Lennart, who, like Zafina, had become very dear to him. And it wasn't just them—Lemar himself had come to Lennart's side, bestowing upon him the honorary title of Citizen of Allcon. As a mark of respect, the Allconians would bow in greeting whenever they saw Lennart, acknowledging his equal status in their society. Lennart had always returned the gesture graciously, earning their admiration.

The cheerful, peaceful human from Earth, who had painted himself like one of their own, had become a beloved figure. Unbeknownst to him, a holographic projection of Lennart, larger than life and in full color, now stood outside the main building, displayed day and night as a tribute. And yet here he lay, fighting for his life.

The medics worked tirelessly to save him. His odds of survival were good, but they warned that a permanent loss of memory could be a lasting consequence of the attack. While one medic operated the tiny robots through wall-mounted monitors, another managed an external device designed to restore brain activity. Using a powerful magnetic apparatus positioned over his head, they stimulated his damaged synapses, analyzing the results in real time on another monitor.

Throughout the procedure, Lennart occasionally jerked uncontrollably as the medics attempted to restore his brain's functionality. Meanwhile, Lennart's mind was lost in an intense dream.

He dreamed of Earth, reliving the most beautiful moments of his childhood. He saw himself as a little boy, being lovingly bathed by his mother after playing in the mud following a rainstorm. He remembered kicking a soccer ball with his father, playing cards with friends, and falling in love for the first time—with the pretty girl who lived in his neighborhood and attended his school. His adventurous school trip abroad came flooding back: sneaking out of his room at night with classmates, undetected by the chaperones. His entire past played out like a fast-forwarded film, each memory warm and vivid.

When the medics finally completed their work, they left Lennart's room, removing their breathing masks as they stepped into the corridor where Zafina and Abron waited. Zafina was about to take over from Abron's shift. The medics informed them that the treatment had been a success. According to Lennart's brainwave readings, nearly all the damaged synapses had been reconstructed. They were optimistic that the remaining few would regenerate over time with the help of the micro-robots left inside Lennart's body.

The anesthetic would soon wear off, and Lennart was expected to recover fully. Relieved, Abron left with the medics, while Zafina stayed behind. She entered Lennart's room and sat beside him, gently stroking his hand as he slept. Her touch radiated a deep, genuine love.

Lennart was still in a deep sleep, his eyes darting rapidly beneath his closed lids as he dreamed. His wound was no longer visible on the outside. Zafina gazed at him and smiled softly—he was still tinted violet from the healing salve. She was hopeful that he would make a full recovery, confident in the healers' extraordinary efforts.

Next to Lennart's bed, on a sleek metallic nightstand, were all the belongings that had been taken from him. His wallet, phone, the stopped wristwatch, and even his folding knife had been carefully placed there. The crumpled shopping bag from a Berlin supermarket, which Lennart had once used as a makeshift breathing device during his first escape attempt, had also been found and returned.

Abron had lovingly arranged these items, ensuring that when Lennart woke up, they would be the first things he saw. The other stolen objects had been returned to their rightful owners by the security team. As for the mischievous birdlike thief, no punishment was given—on Allcon, punishment was not a concept they embraced. Instead, a curfew had been implemented to prevent such incidents from happening again.

If the feathered creature had not been so aggressive, they wouldn't have even considered taking such measures.

On this planet, theft was not punished. No one could go against their nature. Just like on Earth, where certain bird species like ravens, crows, or magpies couldn't resist the urge to collect shiny and metallic objects, this exotic being couldn't either.

Lennart continued dreaming about his past life. Now, he was an adult, recalling the day he bought his computer and 3D printer, and the moment he decided to start his own business. He remembered the intoxicating feeling of freedom. The dream moved further along the timeline, and soon he was sitting by the Todax, blissfully happy. And then... yes, then he dreamed of the beautiful Zafina.

In the dream, it was crystal clear to him that he had fallen head over heels in love with her. While still asleep, he murmured her name. Zafina, who was still sitting beside him and holding his hand, was startled when she heard her name from the dreaming Lennart. She gently stroked his hair.

Lennart woke up, and the first thing he saw was Zafina. He was overjoyed to see her. His head was still a bit foggy, but his thoughts were clear. He sat up on his bed, and as if drawn by a magnet, pulled her close and hugged her tightly, softly repeating her name again and again. He stroked her beautiful face, mesmerized by her stunning eyes. Unable to hold back his emotions, he leaned past her nasal breathing mask and kissed her tenderly on the lips.

Her lips were so soft. Zafina was startled, jerking back to break the kiss. She shook her head and wiped her lips as if to erase the kiss. Lennart hadn't expected such a reaction and felt rejected. Guilt washed over him. Perhaps she didn't feel the same? Or maybe kissing wasn't customary on Allcon? He hoped he hadn't offended her. Bowing his head, he humbly pressed his hands together as if in prayer, hoping she'd understand his gesture and forgive his outburst of emotion.

She waved it off and hugged him tightly. Lennart realized she wasn't angry. Relieved, he closed his eyes and melted into her embrace.

Afterward, she stood up and prepared a bowl of Ulam porridge for him, occasionally slipping a piece of the banana-like fruit into his mouth. Laughing softly, she said, "Ulam-Smusi!" amused by the sound of the word.

"Yes, Ulam Smoothie!" Lennart replied with a grin. He got up and was delighted to see all his missing belongings neatly arranged on his bedside table. He scratched his stubbled chin and decided it was time for a proper shave under the waterfall. Grabbing his pocket watch and folding knife, he headed toward the bathroom. Passing by Zafina, he picked up another piece of the banana-like fruit and pointed toward the waterfall with his index finger to indicate his intention. He felt healthy and, apart from a slight headache, had no lingering effects from his ordeal.

Under the shower, Lennart let the water soak his face, softening his skin. He crushed the banana in his hand and rubbed it over his stubble, using its texture as shaving cream. Opening the pocket watch, he used its reflective surface as a mirror. Then, carefully, he unfolded the pocketknife and began to shave.

Zafina, curious about what Lennart was doing with such mismatched objects, quietly followed him into the bathroom. When she entered, Lennart noticed her presence. Standing naked before her, he felt no embarrassment and continued shaving as if she weren't there.

First, she observed him, studying his body without clothing. Then, drawn by curiosity, she came closer, standing just inches away, watching intently as he carefully shaved. Since male Allconians had no facial hair, Lennart's activity was strange and fascinating to her. He could have just let his beard grow, but his sensitive skin meant he would get a rash if he didn't shave regularly.

When he finished, he washed his face and ran his hand over the smooth skin. Not a single cut. He was relieved to have the right tools for the job.

As Lennart got dressed, Zafina ran her hand over his smooth face. He pointed at the knife, mimed a shaving motion in the air, and said, "Shaving," explaining what he had been doing. Zafina wondered if the process hurt.

"Lennart, shaving… ach? Ach?" she asked, mimicking a pained expression. Lennart shook his head and answered in his own version of Allconian, "Ngo! Lennart shaving ach—ngo!" She smiled at his attempt to speak her language and was relieved to hear it didn't hurt.

Together, they returned to his room. Lennart put his shaving tools back on the table, while Zafina prepared an Ulam starfruit mix for a walk. Lennart handed her another Ulam, gesturing for a larger portion. He longed for a peaceful outing with her, hoping to visit the park where he had first arrived on the planet.

When his fruit cocktail was ready, he drank it all in one go, savoring the taste. Then, like an obedient patient, he sat back on his bed and waited for the fruit's restorative effects to kick in.

As Lennart's blood was sufficiently oxygenated, Zafina took his arm over her shoulder, and they slowly left his habitat together. They walked down the hallway at a leisurely pace, passing the feathered, thieving alien who had nearly killed Lennart with one strike. The creature lay peacefully on its cotton nest. Lennart assumed it was likely nocturnal, as it always seemed to be asleep whenever he passed by during the day.

Since he had been unconscious after the attack, Lennart didn't know much about what had happened afterward, and this left him uneasy. He couldn't shake the fear that the bird-like alien might visit him again at night. Unbeknownst to him, Arbon had locked the creature's enclosure with a security code. Lennart was simply relieved to have his belongings returned to him—shaving with the fruit peeler had been pure torture compared to using Eugen's knife.

They stepped into the elevator and descended two floors. Upon exiting the building through the glass doors, Lennart saw a giant holographic image of himself projected outside. They walked around the projection together, Lennart marveling at the detailed likeness. The hologram stood about five meters tall.

Zafina pointed at the projection and said, "Lennart!" He smiled at her and nodded in agreement. Though Zafina had intended to take a different path, Lennart gestured toward a tall building where he believed the silver statue of Lemar stood. So they strolled along the streets for some time.

Every Allcon resident they passed bowed respectfully to them. Lennart bowed back each time, though he found it a bit exhausting. A gentle breeze blew outside; it was warm, and the sky was a bright shade of orange. There wasn't a single cloud, and neither the massive turquoise moon nor the smaller silver moon was visible.

Above them, aerodynamic flying vehicles zipped past at an incredible speed, about 300 meters overhead. These crafts were the size of Earth cars but emitted no sound from their engines. The only noise was the faint whooshing of air displaced as they moved through the planet's atmosphere—a constant, soft hissing above their heads.

Gradually, they approached the imposing building Lennart had pointed out. He gestured to the statue atop it and asked, "Lemar?" Zafina nodded and responded, though he couldn't understand her words. It confirmed what he suspected—this was indeed Lemar's magnificent residence.

Lennart turned around, trying to locate the park where he had first arrived. He had high hopes that the same place might offer him a way back to Earth. Hastily, he made his way toward the park, pulling Zafina along with him. His recent physical training was beginning to pay off, and with strong, quick strides, they reached the spot.

On the ground lay a circular metal plate, the exact place where Lennart had first opened his eyes on Allcon. He immediately lay down on the plate and said to Zafina, "Earth Lennart Allcon." He rolled and shifted, lying on his back, then on his stomach, then turning in every possible direction. He kept repeating, "Lennart Earth, Lennart Earth!" to make her understand he was looking for a way back to Earth.

Zafina squealed with laughter, shaking her head. She pointed to the ground and said, "Lennart Earth Ngo! Lennart Earth Lemar!" His frantic movements and odd positions made her laugh even harder—he looked endearing in his earnestness.

Lennart, however, wasn't in the mood for laughter. His hopes of finding a way home at this spot were fading fast. There was no mechanism to activate, no obvious path back. The position alone wasn't enough. He sweated with the effort, and when he finally understood that only Lemar could send him back to Earth, he stood up like a man on autopilot. "But how?" he wondered. Surely Lemar had some machine, a counterpart to what existed on Earth, that could help him return.

Zafina gently tugged him back toward the habitat, reminding him that the effects of the Ulam fruit would diminish if they strayed too far from his oxygen-rich room.

The return trip felt strenuous, yet oddly quicker than the journey to the park. The thought that Lemar held the key to his return kept repeating in Lennart's mind. He needed to learn more.

When they reached the habitat building and Lennart still had sufficient oxygen in his blood, he raised his hand and said, "Zafina Lennart Todax!" He was determined to have at least one meaningful conversation with her that day.

Zafina tilted her head in surprise, as though wondering how Lennart knew about the Todax. She mumbled something he couldn't understand but ultimately agreed to accompany him to the top floor.

When they reached the 14th floor, Lennart sat on the ground in the same spot where he had sat before. He patted the floor beside him, inviting Zafina to join him. She sat down next to him. Lennart closed his eyes, calming his mind and spirit.

With heartfelt sincerity, he inwardly called upon the Todax, seeking an audience. His deep and genuine request resonated, and the Todax reached out to him.

He heard the marvelous, soundless resonance.

"Hello, child of Earth, I'm delighted by your visit!" the voice resonated within his consciousness. Lennart responded:

"Dear Todax, I'm grateful that you've answered my call and reached out to me. Today, I am not here alone. My friend Zafina has kindly agreed to accompany me to this meeting. She has helped me so much, doing everything in her power to make my life easier. Without her, I might not even be alive anymore or would be leading a very miserable existence. Would it be possible for both of us to speak with you? Unfortunately, I still understand far too little of the Allconian language. But with your ability to communicate without words, I could convey something very important to Zafina. It concerns my deepest wish to return home. As you surely know, I've tried everything I could to get back, but nothing has worked."

After Lennart finished expressing his thoughts, he suddenly heard Zafina's voice in his consciousness. She spoke:

"My dearest Todax, it is always a joy to merge thoughts with you. Every single time, it enriches me. Lennart, I am amazed by the profound emotions you carry within you. Knowing you without words doesn't reveal this beautiful side of you. I've certainly noticed your efforts to return to your home planet, but it's not as simple as you might imagine. It's not even in my power to send you back.

Here's the thing: we haven't had the best experiences with your kind. You know, Eugen also came to us. Based on his motives, it's difficult to justify simply letting you return. His mission was to bring advanced technology back to your planet to conquer other lands and oppress innocent beings. Your species is not ready yet. Everyone thinks only of their own gain, no matter what happens to others.

Even just your knowledge of our world would awaken the greed of warlords on your planet. Moreover, your body is now infused with our technology, and you would likely become the longest-living human in your planet's history. Believe me, the torments you'd endure as people tried to uncover the secret of your longevity would not be in your best interest.

Our world operates differently. We thrive only as a collective, and we are only as strong as the weakest among us. That's why we make sure that everyone contributes to the well-being of the whole community."

Lennart's hopes faded, and a deep sorrow overcame him. His return home now felt infinitely distant. As he pictured never being able to see his beloved parents or his one true friend again, tears rolled down his face.

Then, Todax spoke again:

"Thank you, Zafina, for your explanation. Lennart, do not despair. I know you are familiar with the behaviors of your people that Zafina described and that you neither came here willingly nor intended to subjugate anyone through technology. You must also understand that even your concept of love differs greatly from true love.

I know you've fallen in love with Zafina and that you're caught in an internal conflict over your return. Humans often tend to want to possess someone they've given their heart to, as though it's only possible to feel genuine love for one person."

Love, by your standards, is a primitive transaction—a contract between two beings. True love, however, is freedom—the will to never limit the one you love. Loyalty doesn't mean loving only one person while shunning all others. That would be like knowing an entire language but being allowed to use only a single word.

The Allconers do not experience such limitations. They feel a profound reverence for life and for the sentient beings around them. Humans kill and consume sentient creatures simply because they find them tasty. When your species evolves further, you will understand that this way of living is not grounded in love for all. One day, you will stop. But until then, the senseless slaughter will continue.

Still, I do not wish to judge you for it. That would be like judging a child for not possessing the knowledge of a top-ranking scientist while it is still learning to walk. For a member of your race, you are quite advanced—further along than many others. But not far enough to be equal to the Allconers. Yet too far advanced to simply be sent back."

This was another blow to Lennart's already fragile hopes. He swallowed hard, feeling utterly powerless. He was at the mercy of Lemar's decisions. There was no way for him to return home on his own. This sense of helplessness gave rise to a deep inner sorrow. His current predicament meant he couldn't live the life he was used to on Earth in this unnatural environment, nor could he return to Earth with his knowledge of Allcon and lead a happy, fulfilling life there.

Moreover, Zafina would not reciprocate his feelings for her. She held an understanding of love that he could not grasp. Desperate, Lennart pleaded:

"You could remove all the technology from my body! I could promise to destroy the machine that brought me here as soon as I return to Earth. I'd do anything—agree to any condition you impose on me. All I want is to go back to my family, my best friend, and to Earth, where I can live a life suited for a human being. Here, I can't even breathe properly without the help of the Ulam fruit."

No sooner had he finished expressing his thoughts than it happened—the effects of the Ulam began to fade, and Lennart found it increasingly difficult to breathe. He was about to thank them for the conversation and say goodbye when a fog slowly enveloped his consciousness. Lennart lost consciousness.

9. Downward Spiral

Felix stood in his bathroom, staring at his reflection in the mirror. He looked disheveled. Dark circles under his eyes and the wild stubble on his face made him recoil at his own appearance. He hadn't left his apartment for days since being fired. Most of the formalities were handled online or over the phone. He had no motivation to do anything.

Thoughts of his former colleagues haunted him, imagining the gossip his dismissal must have stirred. And then, as always, his thoughts circled back to Lennart. There had been no word from the police or anyone else. The only people who stood by him were his loving parents, who called him regularly and listened sympathetically to the injustices he had endured. Felix knew he couldn't keep living like this, but he couldn't find a solution to his situation either. Everything felt meaningless.

His entire worldview, all the principles he'd worked hard to uphold over the years—what was the point of it all? This question burned in his mind. He couldn't bring himself to accept that he had found fulfillment in his work. That he had spent hours, days, weeks, months, and years handling unresolved issues for a company that wasn't even his own, just to see virtual numbers appear in his bank account at the end of every month. Numbers that could be exchanged for colorful pieces of paper to cover his basic needs. The absurdity of it all hit him.

He felt betrayed by the world, robbed of his precious time. And in the end, he'd been discarded over what was nothing more than a delusion. His shoulders sagged. He felt hungry, but mentally, he was miles away from preparing anything proper to eat. His food supplies were running dangerously low, yet he couldn't summon the willpower to go shopping.

He walked into the kitchen and inspected his empty refrigerator. There wasn't even enough for a simple buttered slice of bread. For days, that's all he'd been living on. He asked himself, "There has to be something edible left in this house, right?" One by one, he opened all the cupboards. Eventually, he found an unopened can of corn.

To his surprise, he felt a strange joy at the discovery. Grabbing a spoon and a can opener from the drawer, he eagerly opened the can and began scooping out the sweet corn. When he had fished out the very last kernel, he drank the remaining liquid straight from the can. Setting the empty can down on the kitchen counter with the spoon still inside, he glanced around the room.

His kitchen was a disaster. Dirty dishes piled up, surfaces cluttered, and an overall sense of neglect hung in the air. He felt disgusted, but he did nothing about it. Everyday household chores, which he used to handle automatically, now seemed like insurmountable obstacles.

Physically, he was fine, but there was a deep, inexplicable sickness within him. Yet, he knew he had no choice—he had to go out. His pantry was bare. The trash was piling up, and the smell was beginning to spread.

Felix had always been an organized person before all of this. So, in a bid to regain some semblance of control, he decided to make a plan. He walked into the living room and sat at his desk—though his computer, seized by the police, was still missing. Pulling a blank sheet of paper from the printer and grabbing a pen, he moved to his recliner.

He switched on the TV, letting some meaningless channel play in the background, and began writing down everything he needed to do. Speaking each item aloud as he wrote it, he tried to set himself on a productive course.

"Me: shower, trim nails, shave, brush teeth…"

Every now and then, the TV distracted him. Returning to his list, he wrote: "Kitchen: do the dishes, tidy up, take out the trash, grocery shopping." Just then, an episode of an old TV show he used to enjoy came on. It completely derailed his efforts. While he sat in his armchair, feeling somewhat full and watching the show, he found it surprisingly dull this time. Before he knew it, he drifted off into a food coma.

Nearly two hours later, Felix was startled awake by the obnoxious jingle of a TV commercial. He had been dreaming about Lennart. Without realizing it, his subconscious had blended scenes from the TV show with his dream. In it, he and Lennart were driving together. Lennart was cheerfully at the wheel when another car suddenly crashed into the driver's side. Blood was everywhere. Felix screamed at the top of his lungs in the dream. He woke up drenched in sweat and in a foul mood.

A voice from the infomercial blared out of the TV: "With Lackmagix, even deep scratches from parking accidents disappear! Order today and get a second tube absolutely free!"

The remote control, his pen, and the notepad were now lying on the floor, having fallen there while he slept. Though it was only a dream, Felix's heart was racing, and his dark thoughts quickly returned, taking over his mind once more. He grabbed the phone and dialed the only people who truly understood him—his parents.

His mother answered. Felix poured out his feelings, recounting the horrible dream and the rut he was stuck in. He admitted that he was so unmotivated that he couldn't even muster the energy to go grocery shopping. She listened attentively and urged him to seek help.

"I know a good psychologist," she said. "I'll call and arrange an appointment for you as soon as possible. Don't lose hope, my boy. I can come over and help you tidy up your apartment. I can even stop by the store on my way and pick up some groceries for you."

Embarrassed, Felix politely declined her offer to help with the housework. A few minutes after their conversation ended, the phone rang again. His mother was back on the line. She'd already managed to secure an appointment with the psychologist for the very next morning.

Felix was astonished at how she'd arranged it so quickly, given the notoriously long waiting lists. "Alright," he thought. "It can't hurt to talk to a professional about my situation. Maybe it's not as simple as I think, and perhaps this psychologist can actually help me break free from this vicious cycle."

An hour later, the doorbell rang unexpectedly. Felix hesitated, then cautiously asked through the intercom who was there.

"I've got a pizza delivery for you," came the reply.

Confused, Felix said, "But I didn't order anything!"

With a friendly tone, the pizza delivery guy replied, "The pizza was ordered online by your mother and has already been paid for." Felix cautiously opened the door and accepted the large pizza box along with a soft drink. He thanked the delivery person warmly, then, surprised, called his mother to thank her for her swift help. She had ordered him a giant family-sized four-cheese pizza with extra olives—his favorite. The aroma of the freshly delivered pizza filled the entire apartment. Felix couldn't resist and began devouring it ravenously until he was completely stuffed. He managed to eat half of the family-sized pizza in one go. Then he closed the box, saving the other half for later.

Feeling so full that moving was an effort, he collapsed back into his recliner and turned on the TV. Even though there was nothing worthwhile on, his mood improved slightly. He let himself be passively entertained for hours, repeatedly dozing off and then continuing his TV marathon. This went on late into the evening. By then, he had finished off the rest of the pizza in small bites, eating it cold without even bothering to heat it up. He spent the entire night in his recliner, barely moving, half-asleep and half-awake.

When morning finally came, Felix struggled to pull himself together and managed to take a long shower. Despite his intentions, he didn't trim his long nails or shave. In his rush, he also forgot to brush his teeth. He grabbed some fresh clothes from the closet, got dressed, and left the apartment in a hurry so as not to be late for his doctor's appointment. Before getting into his car, he stopped by the small bakery next to his apartment, grabbing a coffee-to-go and two cream-filled doughnuts for the road.

At the doctor's office, Felix was asked to sit in the waiting room and fill out a form about his current condition. When his turn came, the psychologist listened as Felix recounted everything—starting with Lennart's disappearance, the misunderstanding surrounding his arrest, and finally his dismissal from work. The doctor listened attentively, taking detailed notes, and then said, "Mr. Schulte, from what you've described, it seems you are suffering from a severe depression. The good news is that this condition is treatable. I recommend therapy. If you're open to getting help, I can prescribe it for you. There's a specialized clinic nearby that achieves excellent results with cases like yours."

Felix had expected some advice or perhaps a prescription for medication but hadn't anticipated being referred to a psychiatric facility. The doctor seemed to notice Felix's apprehension and added in a calming voice, "In addition to therapy, I'll prescribe you an antidepressant and some mild sleeping pills to help you relax and finally get a good night's sleep. These are plant-based, not strong, and they take weeks to show effects. Most importantly, they are non-addictive."

Feeling utterly deflated, Felix reluctantly agreed to the doctor's treatment plan. But he didn't feel reassured. "Don't worry, Mr. Schulte," the doctor continued, "This is an open facility. Your stay will be completely voluntary, and depending on your progress, you might soon be able to spend nights at home while continuing therapy during the day."

Felix took the prescriptions and referral papers and headed home. On the way, he stopped at the nearest pharmacy to pick up the medications and then drove to the clinic to complete his admission process. To his surprise, they were able to schedule him for treatment the very next day. "Tomorrow already?" he muttered in astonishment, then calmed himself with the thought, "Well, the sooner, the better."

Exhausted, Felix returned to his apartment. Once home, he called his mother to discuss the doctor's recommendation. He was still unsure whether he should take this step. They spoke at length, and his mother offered him words of encouragement. Following the doctor's instructions, Felix took his medication and tried to mentally prepare for his hospital stay. The whole ordeal had drained him so completely that he felt utterly spent.

But with all the back and forth, he once again forgot about food. "What's wrong with me? I was already outside, and I couldn't even manage to grab some rolls and a piece of cheese!" he grumbled to himself in frustration. He debated whether he should just make it a fasting day to avoid going back out. But he couldn't even muster the will for that. Desperately, he thought, "I never imagined there could be an illness that makes life so miserable, even with a healthy, functioning body. An illness that paints everything in such a grim light."

There was no other way. Felix gathered what little strength he had and decided to go out again. The sun was blazing overhead. Berlin and its surroundings were oppressively hot that day. Every step felt twice as draining as usual. He wanted to prove to himself that he could do it if he really tried. His original plan was to go straight to the nearest supermarket, but he didn't have the energy for that. Instead, he turned into the small bakery right next to his apartment, where he had already bought coffee that morning. The selection was sparse. "Better than nothing," he convinced himself, just to avoid the crowded supermarket. He grabbed two rolls and a pretzel and hurried back to his apartment as fast as he could.

"At least it's something," he thought, feeling a small flicker of pride. Those five minutes had left him drenched in sweat.

Back home, he opened the fridge to grab a refreshing drink, only to be reminded once again that it was empty. Resigned, he let the tap run for a bit to get the coldest water possible, filled a glass, and downed it in one gulp. A loud, satisfied "Ahh" escaped his lips as he lowered the glass. "Wow, that hits the spot," he said aloud to himself. "You've got to stay hydrated in this heat," he reminded himself, promptly pouring a second glass. After quenching his initial thirst, he sipped cautiously from the second glass.

He felt so drained, as if he'd just run a marathon. Carrying the bakery bag and the glass of water, he made his way to the living room. Carefully, he set the food and drink down beside him, collapsed into his recliner, and fell asleep within minutes, not even managing to turn on the TV.

A few hours later, Felix woke up feeling slightly more refreshed. He knew he couldn't relax just yet—he still needed to pack some clothes so he could leave for the clinic early the next morning without any added stress. Like a robot, he got up and began searching through the chaos of his apartment for his gym bag. Unable to find it, he gave up and grabbed a crumpled shopping bag from the kitchen. Then, he haphazardly threw in a few items that would suffice for his first days at the hospital.

He felt oddly detached, as if he were watching himself from the outside. Everything seemed so meaningless. Perhaps it was a side effect of the medication he had taken. "Hmm, but didn't the doctor say the meds wouldn't kick in for weeks?" he wondered, trying to reassure himself. "Felix, it can only get better from here," he told himself firmly.

He tossed the full bag next to his recliner, took a bite of the pretzel, and sipped his water. Settling back into the chair, he turned on the TV. He spent the entire evening and night asleep in the recliner.

The next morning, Felix grabbed his bag of clothes, tucked the rolls under his arm, took his pills with the remaining water from the glass, and stuffed the medicine into the plastic bag along with his clothes. Without showering, changing his clothes, brushing his teeth, or shaving, he headed off to the hospital.

Lennart slowly opened his eyes. He found himself back in his habitat. The soft strains of relaxing music played in the background. Gradually, memories of the conversation with Zafina and the Todax came flooding back. The more he recalled the exchange, the deeper his despair grew. He mentally replayed the entire dialogue over and over. No matter how he tried to twist and turn it, he couldn't see a solution that would allow him to live a life fit for a human.

Lost in thought, time slipped away without a single sign of life from anyone. No Abron, no Zafina—no one. He began to drift into memories. He saw his beloved parents, whose absence he felt so deeply. They would have given their lives to save his. He thought of his friend Felix, whose presence he missed so intensely that it was like a wound in his soul. Felix had always been there for him, a true friend. At the same time, he realized he would never see any of them again. He hadn't even had the chance to say goodbye.

So many kind and heartfelt words were left unsaid, words he longed to share but never could. The weight of it all was unbearable. The more he dwelled on the past, the more an overwhelming sadness took hold of him. Tears welled up in his eyes.

"Damn it," he muttered through his sobs. "Eugen warned me about this, and I refused to believe him. Now he's free." His voice broke as he repeated that final word to himself over and over. "Free. Free. Free."

It became increasingly clear to him that under these circumstances, he simply couldn't go on. He, too, wished for release. He activated the privacy shield, shutting out the world—he didn't want to see or hear anyone. Alone in the silence, his mind began to churn through various ways to end his miserable existence with as little suffering as possible.

He could fashion a noose from the remnants of Eugen's clothing and hang himself. He could take the knife and drive it into his heart or slash his wrists. Alternatively, he could step outside without eating the Ulam fruit, find a hiding spot, and hope no one would find him. Or perhaps it would be better to consume the Ulam fruit after all—then he'd have more time to locate the perfect hiding place and let himself suffocate from lack of oxygen, just as had nearly happened several times before.

10. Freedom Fighter

Lennart sat motionless for hours, his thoughts circling endlessly around the same question: how could he stay true to himself while finding a way forward? Silent tears streamed down his face as he reflected on the events that had brought him to this moment. He looked at his arms and noticed how the violet hue on his skin had begun to fade, a bittersweet reminder of his journey.

All attempts to return home had failed. A life where he couldn't breathe freely was inconceivable. The thought of existing for decades as some sort of exhibit was unbearable. Yet giving up wasn't an option. Deep down, he felt a resilience he needed to hold onto.

He spoke his thoughts aloud, piecing together the reasons that had led to his predicament:

"Love, which they claim I cannot understand? Maybe that's true. But it doesn't mean I don't value it. Technology that must be protected to keep it from falling into the wrong hands? That makes sense, and I'd do anything to play my part." The arguments, which had seemed absurd before, now carried a certain weight.

Lennart resolved not to give in. He gathered his and Eugen's personal belongings, carefully placing them into a crumpled bag.

"I won't just move forward; I'll preserve what I've learned," he whispered to himself. It wasn't just his decision anymore—it felt like a commitment to take responsibility for his path.

With a clear mind, he prepared for what lay ahead. He took fruits from the bowl, rinsed an empty bottle under the room's fountain, and filled it with the puree he had prepared.

"This is hard, but I'll get through it," he thought, as a strange calm began to settle over him.

Lying on his cot, he thought of his parents and was overwhelmed by a sense of gratitude. In his mind, he embraced them and whispered:

"Mom, Dad, you are the best parents any child could ask for. You taught me strength, and I'll carry that strength with me wherever this road leads."

He also said an imaginary farewell to Felix, thanking him for everything they'd shared.

"Felix, my friend, out of the billions of people on Earth, you are my one true friend. Thank you for always being there, for your help, your listening ear, and the laughter we shared. I'll never forget those moments. Have a wonderful, fulfilling life!"

After wiping the tears from his cheeks, Lennart knew the time was nearing. He stood, deactivated the privacy screen briefly to check the corridors for visitors, then left the glass wall transparent to not miss the right moment. Dusk was falling on Allcon, and it would take another one or two hours before the timing was perfect. The agonizing wait was becoming unbearable.

He decided to pass the time with one final act of comfort for himself. He stood under the refreshing cascade of the waterfall shower, hoping the sensation would soothe him and ease the weight on his heart. As the water flowed over him, he went over his plan in his mind. After drying off and dressing slowly, he resolved to leave no trace behind. Back in his room, he cleaned the mortar thoroughly, put the fruit bowl back in its place, and tucked the prepared bottle into the bag.

He sat cross-legged on the cot, folded his hands, and closed his eyes. Though not religious, he began a quiet prayer, more like a child's direct plea to the universe:

"Dear God, if you're real, forgive me for lacking the strength to endure my life in this glass terrarium. I only ask one thing: please don't let me suffer for long."

Opening his eyes slowly, Lennart inspected the corridor again. Once the last visitor had passed, he pulled the bag close to him with his foot. He felt the moment had come. Even if he encountered a few of Allcon's inhabitants in the halls or outside, he was confident they wouldn't hinder his plan.

He unscrewed the cap of the bottle, took a few deep breaths, and drank the fruit puree in one go. Without hesitation, he sealed the empty bottle and placed it in the bag. He waited for the effects to set in, then grabbed the bag and headed purposefully toward the airlock.

As he stepped into the hallway, he glanced briefly at the feathered ape-being's enclosure, shaking his head.

"If only you'd hit harder, I'd have been freed long ago," he muttered. Without delay, he walked to the elevators, descended to the ground floor, and slipped outside.

Once outdoors, he paused. He was startled to see a holographic projection of himself towering over the habitat's entrance. The three-dimensional image was larger than life, and he frowned at it in frustration.

"Well, Lennart, you idiot, let them keep your 3D likeness in their glass tube and gawk at it all they want. Not me!" His irritation gave him a sense of determination, propelling him forward.

He walked briskly toward the park, the anti-gravity vehicles silently gliding above him. Despite the late hour, the sky was aglow—not only from the artificial lights of the floating cars and streetlamps but also from the two moons reflecting the light of their sun. He sighed, disappointed.

"Complete darkness? Not a chance. The sky's full of stars and colorful nebulae," he thought bitterly.

The illuminated surroundings made his plan more challenging. As he made his way, several Allcon residents passed by, politely bowing. Lennart returned the gesture with a forced smile each time, trying to appear inconspicuous. Inwardly, his tension grew.

Clutching the bag tightly, he repeated to himself, "Just don't draw attention!" His sweat-soaked palms gripped the bag as he pressed on through the exhausting walk. His heart pounded, but he didn't stop.

When Lemar's palace came into view, brightly lit and crowned by its imposing statue, Lennart steeled himself.

"Not much further. Almost there. Just hold on," he told himself.

As he neared the park, he searched for a suitable hiding place, but every potential spot seemed too exposed. A soft breeze tousled his hair, but sweat continued to bead on his temples. Concentrating intensely, he scanned the area—no secluded corners, no quiet niches. Nothing seemed adequate.

Time was against him. The park loomed ahead, shrouded in a dim nocturnal haze. At first, unease gripped him, but as he entered, it transformed into genuine fear. His sad reflections turned into grim resolve as he took his first steps into the night-draped park.

Purposefully, he veered off the paved path toward a denser part of the park. He kept glancing back to ensure no one was following or watching where he was heading. Unfortunately, there were no bushes in the park where he could lie down unnoticed. The ground was covered in soft moss, from which large, sprawling trees emerged. He tried breaking off a few branches he could reach from the ground, but the tree resisted his efforts. Sweat began pouring down his face, and desperation started creeping in.

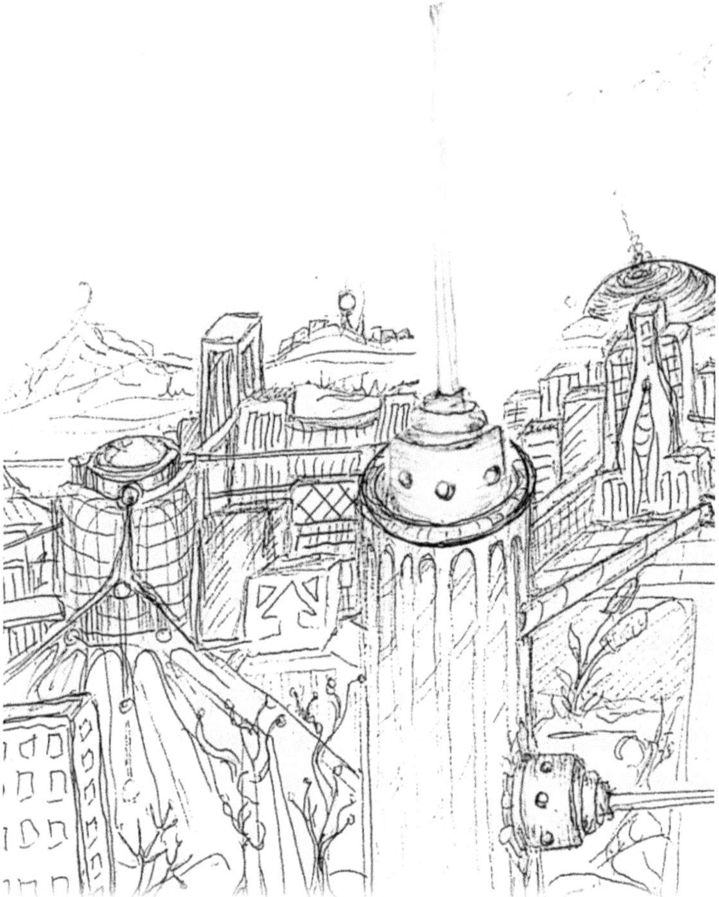

Then, an idea struck him: he could use Eugen's sharp pocketknife from the bag. To get to the leafy branches, though, he'd have to climb the tree—there was no other way. Reluctantly, he left the bag at the base of the trunk and clenched the knife between his teeth to free both hands for climbing. The hardest part was reaching the first branch, but the others grew densely above it.

He climbed about three meters high and began using the knife to quickly hack away at the branches, separating them from the tree. Impatience got the better of him at times; he'd partially cut through a branch and then snap it off by hand to save time. The severed branches fell to the ground below. When he had gathered enough, he folded the knife, clenched it between his teeth again, and carefully maneuvered back down to the lowest sturdy branch before jumping to the ground.

The landing was painful—due to the planet's increased gravity, he weighed significantly more than on Earth. He paused, grimacing as sharp pain shot through his feet. Every step hurt. It took several minutes before the burning sensation subsided enough for him to move again. Satisfied with his progress, he tossed the pocketknife back into the bag.

Gathering the branches from the ground, he piled them beside the tree, close to where the bag rested. He quickly lay down flat on his back next to the heap and pulled the colorful bag close to his side. Then he began covering himself with the branches, one by one, working as quickly as his trembling hands allowed.

Suddenly, he froze mid-motion. As he was about to place another branch on top of himself, a bright green, glowing creature leaped from the branch onto his hand. Startled, he recoiled slightly. The creature resembled a spider, but its numerous legs radiated out from its small, round body like the rays of a tiny sun—about sixteen legs stretched out in all directions.

To his own surprise, Lennart calmed down quickly and spoke to the insect.

"Hey, sun spider, let's strike a deal. You can bite, sting, or eat me—whatever you like—but please wait until I'm gone first."

The odd serenity in his voice amazed him. Gently, he placed the creature next to him and resumed covering himself with branches.

When he finally finished, exhausted to his core, only his eyes were left uncovered, gazing upward. Waiting for the fruit's effects to fully take hold, he watched the majestic sight of the two moons dominating the sky. Every minute dragged on, feeling like an eternity. In his mind, he said his final goodbyes to everyone he loved.

A final prayer escaped his lips:

"Dear God in heaven, please, let it happen now."

Breathing became harder with every passing moment. He knew the time had come. His body grew weaker, and his vision blurred. As the world faded away, he reached beneath the branches for the leather cord around his neck, where the key to his freedom hung. He clutched it tightly in his hand as his consciousness began to slip.

Everything became quiet. A profound darkness enveloped his existence. Then, his grip loosened, and the key fell from his hand to the ground beside his lifeless body.

In the meantime, Felix sat apathetically in a semicircle in a large therapy room, dulled by the medication he had been given. There were eight patients in the group, all showing similar symptoms. One by one, they introduced themselves and shared their struggles in detail. When it was Felix's turn, he spoke:

"Hi, I'm Felix, and I suffer from severe depression. It all started when my best friend suddenly disappeared overnight. It's presumed he's no longer alive. His empty car was found at the edge of a forest, but despite search efforts, the police came up empty-handed. I was overzealous and tried to help the officers with their search, but then I was taken into custody under suspicion for no reason. After they turned my apartment upside down, all the so-called evidence they found proved to be baseless.

During the investigation, the police also contacted my employer, which resulted in me being abruptly fired out of fear of bad publicity. Other than my family, everyone I know has distanced themselves from me. Because of this, my life has felt utterly pointless. My mom suggested I seek medical treatment since all I do these days is eat and sleep. And now, here I am."

Felix's tone was devoid of emotion. The other participants clapped for him and showed visible empathy. After the session, Felix returned to his room. It was technically a two-bed room, but for now, he had it to himself. The hospital was likely not at full capacity, which explained how quickly his admission had been arranged.

Later, dinner was delivered. It tasted awful, but in his current state, Felix didn't care. Early in the evening, his parents came to visit, bringing him snacks and fresh clothes. When his mother noticed how overgrown Felix's fingernails had become, she reached into her handbag and silently clipped them for him within minutes. She told him about the chaos she'd encountered while collecting his belongings from his apartment and how she had tidied everything up, even taking out the trash because the heat had made the whole place reek.

In a calm and reassuring tone, she said: "Your apartment is clean and orderly again, so you can focus on getting better. Oh, and something surprising happened, but I'll tell you more about it tomorrow."

Felix was so grateful he kissed her forehead without a word.

When his parents left that evening, the night nurse came in at the same time. In a firm tone, she handed him a small measuring cup. "Good evening, Mr. Schulte, I'm Nurse Karin. Here are your meds for tonight. Down the hatch—one, two, three!"

Felix took the cup, which contained two tablets. She stood motionless, waiting until he swallowed them in her presence. Once he complied, she wished him a good night, turned off the ceiling light, and left, closing the door behind her. Only the soft glow of his bedside lamp remained.

The pills soon made him drowsy and killed his appetite. He didn't touch the snacks his parents had brought, even though he would normally have torn into the chocolate-covered butter cookies, a childhood favorite. He kept turning over his mother's cryptic comment about the "surprise." It wasn't like her to be so secretive. Surely, it had nothing to do with Lennart's disappearance. Maybe his ex-boss had reached out, or perhaps an old coworker had run into her.

But sleep overcame him quickly, and he drifted into a deep slumber.

The next morning, Felix was rudely awakened by the morning nurse shouting, "Breakfast!" as he entered the room. Felix still had no appetite.

"Good morning, Mr. Schulte! Sleep well? How are we feeling today? What would you like for breakfast—bread with cheese or ham?" the nurse asked.

Reluctantly, Felix replied, "Honestly, I'm not hungry."

The nurse, understanding, offered to leave the tray for later, in case his appetite returned. Then he left the room.

Felix felt drained—the pills were taking a toll on him. It was as if he had been doing hard labor all night. Still, he managed to pull himself out of bed and headed for the shower, his mind wandering. "Usually, a good shower helps wake me up."

But even the refreshing sensation of the water did nothing to shake off his deep lethargy. He slowly put on his tracksuit, deciding to take a short walk around the hospital grounds.

By early morning, it was already quite warm outside. The secluded hospital grounds were clean, well-maintained, and dotted with bushes and flower beds. What started as a peaceful, idyllic stroll quickly turned into a "freak show." Felix felt a wave of unease when he encountered some patients from other wards.

A young man, about Felix's age, wrapped in a hospital gown, silently followed him step for step. Whenever Felix stopped walking, the man stopped as well. This odd shadow finally left him alone when another patient walked past, drawing the gown-clad man's attention and prompting him to start trailing the new target instead.

Not far from the smoking area, another confused patient stood yelling profanities at a trash can. "Oh God, what kind of place have I ended up in? Mom, get me out of here!" Felix mumbled to himself, overwhelmed, and quickly headed back inside, desperate to retreat to the quiet of his room.

Once there, he shut the door behind him as if trying to escape to a protective island amid chaos. He sat on his bed, staring at the breakfast tray that still hadn't been cleared away. He had no appetite. Among the bread and toppings sat a small cup of fruit yogurt. He picked it up, shaking the plastic container a few times to mix it well before peeling back the foil lid. Without bothering to use a spoon, he drank the yogurt straight from the cup.

A soft knock interrupted him. Before he could say "Come in," the door slowly creaked open. Felix's eyes widened in surprise. He wasn't expecting this.

There she was.

He quickly lowered the yogurt cup, setting it on the table. "Nicole? What a surprise!" he exclaimed. She hesitated at the doorway but soon stepped inside, breaking into a giggle. Felix had a yogurt mustache.

She tried to stay serious but couldn't manage it. "Hi, Felix. You've got a little something on your upper lip," she teased. Felix wiped the yogurt off his face and chuckled briefly.

"I hope I'm not interrupting. I called your house earlier and spoke to your mom. She told me you were here," Nicole explained, sitting down next to him on the bed. Felix suddenly realized this must have been the "unexpected news" his mother had mentioned yesterday.

Felix began recounting everything that had happened to him. Nicole stayed for about an hour, listening.

As they talked, he couldn't help but think back to that evening at the café with her and Evelyn. Feeling a surge of closeness, he shifted a little nearer to her. But he quickly noticed her discomfort. She pulled away slightly and said, "Listen, Felix, I'm sorry, but this is all too much for me. First Lennart's disappearance, then the uncomfortable questions from the police, and now you being here… in a mental hospital. It's just overwhelming. I can't handle it, and I need some time to process everything. I hope you understand."

Felix nodded silently. Nicole stood up and said only, "Take care," as she left, closing the door behind her.

Tears welled up in his eyes, but he fought hard not to cry. Clenching his fists tightly, he tried to suppress the pain surging through him. He sat motionless, staring into the void. This was an experience he wished he could have avoided altogether.

11. Judgment

A violent spasm shot through Lennart's entire body. His eyes snapped open. Slowly, he began to realize that his plan had failed. He was lying flat on his back, pinned down by the planet's gravity to a smooth, rock-hard table. When he tried to sit up, he discovered that he couldn't move. He attempted to lift his head, but that too was impossible. From the corner of his eye, he saw two Allconers standing nearby. To his horror, he realized that his head, torso, arms, and legs were securely restrained to the table.

His mind burned with the question of how they had found him—and where he was now. It was clear he wasn't in his habitat anymore. The room was far larger than his glass tube. Metallic, polished pipes crisscrossed the space, gleaming under the lights. Faint hissing noises escaped from the pipes, blending with the constant hum of a synthetic voice speaking in the background. He couldn't understand the words, but the language was unmistakably that of the planet's inhabitants.

A deep unease began to wash over him. The helplessness of being unable to move was compounded by the fact that he wasn't getting enough oxygen from the air around him. Panic began to take hold. He started to scream, his voice cracking with desperation as the constriction in his chest worsened. His head was immobilized by a metallic ring that pressed his forehead against the flat surface of the table.

One of the Allconers approached him and pressed a device against his neck. There was a sharp hiss, followed by a slight pressure, and suddenly he could breathe again. The relief was immediate, but the terror remained. Lennart's eyes darted wildly around the room—the only part of his body he could still move. He was desperate to figure out where he was. Judging by his surroundings, he guessed he might be in some sort of medical treatment room.

Fear surged through him. He was entirely at the mercy of these two alien beings. Were they treating him because they had revived him? Or was he here as punishment for trying to escape?

Determined to break free, he gathered every ounce of strength he had, clenching his fists and yanking his limbs against the restraints. But the metal bands around his arms and legs held fast.

"Help! Let me go! I want out of here!" he shouted uncontrollably.

The two presumed medics didn't react. Instead, one of them stepped closer and began speaking to him in a calm, steady tone. Lennart, of course, couldn't understand a word. The Allconer gestured with its hands, seemingly trying to indicate that he should calm down. Meanwhile, the other held a hose-like device over Lennart's abdomen.

A strange tingling sensation coursed through his body. It felt as if something was being pulled out of him. He couldn't know it, but the microscopic robots that had once saved his life were now being extracted from his system.

The sensation went on for what felt like an eternity. Gradually, the tingling subsided and finally stopped altogether. The hose was removed. With a loud clank, all the metal restraints around his body simultaneously released.

Cautiously, Lennart began to move, testing his limbs as if to confirm he was still in one piece. Relieved to find himself unharmed, he slowly sat up. A wave of dizziness washed over him, and his vision blurred for a moment. His heart pounded in his chest, as if it might leap out at any second.

He glanced around frantically, trying to make sense of his surroundings. The room had no windows, only a single door without a handle.

"Probably one of those automatic doors, like at the main entrance to the habitat," he mused. "The kind that opens when you get close enough."

The room was filled with large machines equipped with digital monitors. The screens displayed a human silhouette, surrounded by blinking symbols in the Allconers' language. It reminded him of the displays in his own quarters, but on a much larger scale.

So many questions raced through his mind. What had they sprayed into his neck that allowed him to breathe here without eating the Ulam fruit? Neither of the Allconers wore breathing apparatuses. Who had found him in the park?

The flood of unanswered questions left him reeling, but one thing was certain: he was far from safe.

Was he already dead?

If so, how long had it been? And most importantly, how had they managed to bring him back to life? Or was it the miraculous technology inside him since the attack by the feathered ape-man? So many questions, and not a single answer.

Carefully, he tried to stand up, placing his feet on the ground. His calf brushed against the bag containing his belongings. He only wanted to get up and leave this strange place. Slowly, he managed to rise, though his legs were unsteady and he had a hard time keeping his balance. The two inhabitants of the planet were at his side in an instant, supporting him as if they instinctively knew what he was going through.

Step by step, with their help, he walked two slow laps around the examination table. Gradually, the dizziness subsided. The automatic door hissed open, and a self-driving chair rolled into the room. It was sturdy and ergonomically designed. Lennart was gently lowered into the chair. One of the two picked up his crumpled bag from the floor and placed it on his lap as the automated wheelchair began to move toward the exit.

The two beings walked alongside him at the same steady pace. Another door slid open on its own, and they entered a long, sterile corridor. On both sides, at regular intervals, were closed doors. At the far end of the corridor was another door and a sharp turn branching off in both directions.

The journey down the hallway felt like it took forever, as the wheelchair moved very slowly. Neither of the Allconers spoke—not to Lennart, nor to each other.

"More uncertainty," Lennart thought bitterly. He still didn't know what they wanted from him or where they were taking him. He whispered to himself, "They're probably taking me back to my habitat from the medical station, just like they've always done."

When they reached the end of the hallway, the group paused in front of the door. It opened automatically, and Lennart slowly rolled into a large room. The two Allconers remained behind, standing at the doorway.

The room Lennart entered left him breathless. It was enormous, with ceilings that seemed impossibly high. It reminded him of a courtroom.

At the center of the room, elevated on a platform, sat King Lemar. On either side of him stood his guards. Below the platform sat Zafina and Abron, their faces neutral yet serious. Surrounding the room was a circular gallery filled to capacity. Every seat was occupied.

Above King Lemar's platform was a spherical glass cabin housing a speaker or moderator. His voice boomed throughout the hall, accompanied by dramatic gestures as he spoke.

Negative thoughts surged through Lennart's mind. Am I being judged? Sentenced? His heart pounded, and fear gripped him. The uncertainty of what awaited him made him tremble all over.

Though his failed suicide attempt had dulled his fear of death, the thought of a slow and agonizing demise terrified him.

The speaker finally fell silent, and an oppressive stillness filled the room. Lennart froze, paralyzed by fear. The silence dragged on for minutes, so heavy that you could have heard a pin drop.

Then King Lemar stood and bowed to the crowd. Instantly, the entire audience rose to their feet and returned the gesture. Lennart, seeing this, stood and bowed as well—thankfully, because all eyes turned to him the moment the greeting ended.

As the crowd sat down in silence, Lennart collapsed back into his chair like a sack of potatoes. His knees were weak, trembling uncontrollably, and his throat was so dry that swallowing became painful.

King Lemar began to speak. Unlike his visit to Lennart's habitat, there were no flashes of cameras this time. The room was silent and attentive, every face serious and still.

Lennart could not discern a single emotion from the faces of the audience. Lemar, however, showed plenty. His arms moved constantly as he spoke, and his face displayed a range of emotions. His tone shifted from soft to loud, his speech alternating between rapid and deliberate.

To Lennart, the wait felt like an eternity. The speech went on for a good half-hour. When Lemar finally finished, the audience began snapping their fingers—a sound Lennart interpreted as their version of applause, much like humans rapped their knuckles on tables after a good lecture.

As the snapping subsided, the speaker in the glass sphere resumed talking. This time, his sentences were brief. Gradually, hands began to rise throughout the room—including those of Lemar, Zafina, and Abron.

"They're voting on something," Lennart thought nervously. "It's official. I've been sentenced. They'll either lock me in that glass tube forever or execute me."

The speaker's voice rang out again, followed by a second round of voting. This time, the few who hadn't raised their hands before did so.

Once more, the speaker spoke briefly, and the room erupted into murmurs as the crowd began talking all at once.

While the voices swirled around him, Lennart's automatic wheelchair began to move. With a gentle swerve, it turned and rolled toward the door through which he had entered.

At the exit, the two Allconers were still waiting, resuming their role as escorts as they walked alongside him. The group turned down the right-hand corridor. The serum sprayed on his neck was beginning to wear off, and breathing became increasingly difficult again. The dizziness returned as well. His breaths grew louder and more strained. Before he could draw attention to his worsening condition, one of his escorts sprayed another dose of the same substance on the skin of his neck. Instantly, his breathing improved, and the spinning sensation started to fade again.

He couldn't stop wondering what was going to happen to him. His thoughts swirled chaotically, but the prevailing feeling was despair. He was hopeless. "The conversation with Zafina and the Todax went terribly. There's no way they're sending me back. Either they're taking me back to the glass habitat or they're going to kill me now!" The thought terrified him, and his shoulders slumped. His gaze dropped, and he clutched the bag on his lap tightly out of fear.

The slow pace of the wheelchair, coupled with the silent escorts, was driving him mad. With every passing meter, with every passing minute, his hopelessness deepened. Not understanding their language, not knowing what had just been decided about him, made the waiting unbearable. His hands trembled so much that his grip on the bag went unnoticed. His legs felt weak, and he realized that if he had to stand up on his own, he wouldn't be able to. "How did it all come to this? That stupid car breakdown, that damn Nazi bunker! Such a coward I am. Any other decision would've gotten me out of this mess. But no, I had to take the shortcut through the woods!" He cursed himself for letting fear of the dark and a few measly mosquitoes drive him to make the worst decision of his life. The corridor stretched on for another 15 meters, but the wheelchair stopped in front of a side door to his right. Lennart looked questioningly at his escorts, who also paused for a moment. The door opened automatically, and the wheelchair rolled inside. Together, the three of them entered the room. Shortly after the door shut behind them, the chair came to a halt again.

Lennart looked around. This wasn't the habitat. Instead, he found himself in another windowless room. Once again, there were massive machines, and he was clearly in another laboratory. This room looked entirely different from the one he'd been in before. The two Allconers gestured for him to get out of the chair. The gravity weighed heavily on his knees. Shaking, he tried to stand but nearly collapsed back into the seat. Finally, the two of them grabbed him under his arms and helped him up. In the process, his bag fell to the floor, but he didn't care.

In the center of the room was a glass tube that resembled a coffin. It was split down the middle, with the top half propped open on metallic hinges. The tube rested on a trapezoidal stand humming softly with electricity. Directly in front of it stood another device resembling an MRI machine, perfectly sized to fit the glass tube inside.

The room was divided in two by a transparent panel, separating it into a laboratory area and an observation section. Lennart was positioned in front of the glass tube and told to climb inside. Overcome with fear, he was incapable of complying. Overpowering him with ease, one of the Allconers lifted him and placed him into the open tube. As this happened, Lennart noticed Lemar, Zafina, and Abron entering the observation area. Paralyzed with terror, he didn't resist as they laid him in the glass container.

At the same time, the other Allconer retrieved Lennart's bag from the floor and placed it near his feet. Slowly, the glass lid lowered automatically and sealed with a faint, airtight thud. Then, silence. He felt only a faint vibration as the glass tube began sliding into the machine. Claustrophobia set in, and he pressed his palms against the lid, but it wouldn't budge. He was breathing loudly and sweating. His heart pounded as the interior grew darker.

A 3D projection appeared inside the tube, showing the observation area. He saw three solemn faces—Zafina on the left, Lemar in the middle, and Abron on the right. Lemar's lips moved as though he was speaking, but Lennart heard nothing. Then he saw tears rolling down Zafina's cheeks as she waved at him with a sorrowful expression, bidding him farewell. They all bowed in unison, and the projection faded to black.

In the oppressive darkness, Zafina's tearful face burned itself into his memory. Panic surged through him. He clasped his hands over his stomach in a desperate prayer and whimpered to himself, "Please, God, have mercy. Don't let me die in pain." He repeated the plea over and over, unable to think clearly.

His adrenaline spiked. He didn't scream or thrash, just clenched his eyes shut and prayed incessantly. The machine began working more intensely, and the vibrations grew stronger. An electric charge built up around him, and his hair stood on end. The last thing he felt was a deafening crack and the searing pain of a lightning bolt coursing through every cell in his body.

12. Assistance

It felt like only a few moments had passed. He had no idea how much time had actually gone by, but when he finally broke free from his paralyzing shock, he found himself staring into the darkness at Zafina's sorrowful face. Slowly, he began to realize that he was still alive. A familiar yet unpleasant smell filled his nostrils—it was stale and musty, like stepping into an antique shop from the street.

He was lying comfortably on his back. Everything around him was silent. Yet somehow, it all felt eerily familiar. Reaching out with both hands, he felt the surface beneath him and understood—he was lying on the leather examination table in the middle of the Nazi bunker.

With a jolt, he leapt up, desperate to get as far as possible from the range of that hellish machine. In his haste, his bag of belongings tumbled to the floor, and he nearly fell down the three steps that led off the platform where the table stood. At the last moment, he managed to steady himself. He couldn't believe his luck.

"They took pity on me and sent me home. Thank God, I'm back home!" he shouted joyfully into the room.

The space wasn't completely dark—soft morning light filtered through the ventilation hatch. It was the same hatch he had fallen through when he stumbled into the bunker while seeking shelter in the nighttime woods. A smile spread across his face as he whispered, "Zafina, my dear, you gave me freedom. I'll always be grateful to you for this."

The machines that had catapulted him to Allcon were all turned off. Carefully, he moved around the room, making sure not to accidentally activate any levers that could bring the devices back to life. Despite his relief at being back on Earth, he was still trapped in this dreadful Nazi bunker. Not wanting to waste any time, he resolved to find something he could use to climb back up to the ventilation hatch and escape.

Cautiously, he approached a large, wardrobe-sized machine positioned next to the ventilation opening. He tried with all his might to push it into place, but it wouldn't budge. It wasn't just too heavy—it was bolted securely to the wall and floor. Undeterred, Lennart considered his options and turned toward a smaller control panel in the corner of the room. If he could push that in front of the hatch and climb onto it, it might give him just enough height to pull himself out to freedom.

On Earth's gravity, his body felt light, almost frail. Frustrated, he discovered that the panel was also bolted down, and he had no tools to loosen the large bolts holding it in place. Slowly, a tingling sensation began to rise in his body. The oxygen still coursing through his bloodstream from the last injection heightened his every breath.

Panic set in immediately. Wild thoughts raced through his mind: "I finally made it back to Earth, only to die miserably here! A prisoner of a regime that doesn't even exist anymore. No, no—I want to be free! Freedom. Nazis. Freedom!"

Like a bolt of lightning, he suddenly remembered the key Eugen had given him as his "key to freedom." Tugging on the leather cord around his neck, he held it tightly in his hand and strode, almost hypnotized, toward the heavy, gray, locked metal door. His hands clenched into fists, his lips pressed tightly together. Trembling, he struggled to fit the key into the lock. It took several attempts, but at last, the key turned. With great effort, he unlocked the mechanism and slowly pushed the handle down.

Before he could even glance beyond the door, the heavy metal swung open with a deafening crash, hurling him to the ground. A cloud of dust and debris surged several meters into the room. Fortunately, Lennart was flung far enough to avoid being crushed by the falling concrete slabs.

Shaken but unharmed, he lay on the floor for a while, stunned by what had just happened. Slowly, his body began to respond again, and he got to his feet, bewildered, trying to make sense of the scene. The dust gradually settled, and Lennart cautiously approached the pile of rubble.

The door had been blasted wide open, but behind it was nothing but a mountain of twisted debris and steel beams, crisscrossing chaotically.

"Oh no—no way I'm getting through there," he muttered under his breath, shaking his head slowly.

What had once been a hallway was now completely blocked, and without heavy equipment, there was no chance of clearing a path. The only escape route he could think of was to use the rubble to build a makeshift staircase up to the ventilation hatch. The only obstacle, however, was his cramped and trembling hands, which severely limited his ability to maneuver.

But thanks to his three daily strength exercises in the habitat and the fact that the high gravity on Allcon now worked to his advantage, he was able to lift even large chunks of concrete with his hands. Without hesitation, he began pushing the largest pieces of rubble against the wall in front of the opening. There was plenty of material at his disposal now. Layer by layer, he painstakingly built a pyramid out of the debris.

Time and again, he climbed to the highest point to check whether it was already tall enough to reach freedom. The higher he went, the shakier the structure became. He still needed to build at least another meter upwards. Most of the material inside the room was already used up. He knew it was dangerous to try to remove loose debris from the hallway beyond. Any piece he dislodged could bring tons of rubble crashing down on him.

Cautiously, he used his right foot to sweep aside smaller stones near the door to make it possible to close it again. Sharp-edged fragments cut into his foot, but in his state of excitement, it didn't even occur to him to put on the sports shoes that were lying in a bag next to the cot. After several painful minutes of sweeping, the door could finally be shut again. He intended to use it as a shield.

Carefully, with the door in front of him, he pulled a few more pieces of rubble out of the pile, his cramped hand clenched into a fist. A few rusty, bent iron bars also tumbled into the room. Hours passed as Lennart painstakingly completed his structure. Finally, he climbed cautiously to the top of his makeshift staircase.

He was ready to abandon everything and crawl out of the bunker into freedom when, in his mind's eye, he suddenly saw Zafina's sorrowful face.

"I know, Zafina, my love, I still owe you this," he said with sudden determination as he climbed back down. Barefoot, he swept debris aside from the path to the door, locked it with the key, and hung the leather cord back around his neck. Then, picking up one of the rusted iron bars lying around, he furiously and indiscriminately began smashing the control panels of the Nazi machinery.

He kept battering the equipment until he felt it was thoroughly destroyed. Exhausted, he picked up his bag from the floor and climbed back to the top of the pyramid. First, he pushed his bag into the open air, and with the last of his strength, he scrambled out of the bunker and into the daylight.

The feeling was indescribable. A wave of love and gratitude flooded through him—love for everything, for every grain of sand on the ground, for every leaf on every tree. The tingling sensation in his body grew stronger as his muscles tightened further, especially in his hands and lips. The excess oxygen coursing through his veins was overwhelming.

Acting on instinct, he sealed the ventilation opening by arranging the wild weeds and picking up fallen leaves from the forest floor to cover the gaps completely. From the outside, there was no longer any sign of the bunker's existence. To mark the spot, however, he lifted three large stones with his cramped hands and stacked them about five meters in front of the hidden entrance.

Though he wanted to run, exhaustion made that impossible. Barefoot, he set off at a slow, steady pace, heading wherever his instincts led him. His hyperventilation made it hard to think clearly, but the wonderful scent of the forest and the birdsong filled him with joy—he felt like the happiest man alive. To ease his cramps, he reassured himself aloud:

"Soon enough, the effects of the oxygen spray will wear off. I just have to hold on a little longer. Mother, Father, Felix—hold on, I'm almost there!"

It was a truly beautiful summer day. By late morning, the warmth was just right. Lennart continued walking resolutely through the forest, sure that he would eventually reach civilization. Without pausing even to put on his shoes, he trudged barefoot through the leaves.

After about half an hour of walking, still lightheaded from the excess oxygen, he spotted a jogger about 100 meters away.

His heart was racing, and he shouted as loudly as he could with his cramped lips, "Hollo! Pleez wate fo mee! I neef helf!"

She stopped for a moment and saw Lennart running toward her. He waved his hand, holding a stuffed bag, and kept repeating those garbled phrases. As he got closer—about 20 meters away—she could see him more clearly. A man painted in bright purple, wearing a white robe, his fingers clenched into fists, and shouting incomprehensible gibberish, wildly waving a shopping bag.

Fear took hold of her, and she ran as fast as she could. Lennart chased after her as best he could. But she was clearly in better physical shape and had far superior endurance from her regular jogging. She ran down a well-trodden forest path, pulling further and further ahead of him.

Even as the distance between them grew, she took her phone from her pocket and, still running, called emergency services. A calm female voice on the other end answered, "This is the police emergency line. What's your emergency?"

Between gasps for air, the jogger introduced herself, gave her location, and explained frantically, "I need help! There's a completely insane guy chasing me through the forest. He must be crazy—he's painted all over in bright purple, wearing a white robe, barefoot, screaming nonsense, and flailing a bag around. Please, I'm terrified!"

The dispatcher reassured her, saying, "Understood! Keep running south toward the main road. I'm sending a patrol your way immediately. They'll be there in just a few minutes. Hang up so you can focus on running toward them!"

Lennart could only see the jogger disappearing in the distance, but he didn't give up—it was a matter of life and death. However, his weakened state wasn't helping. The deeper he breathed as he ran, the more oxygen flooded his body. His fists throbbed with pain from being clenched so tightly. He was on the brink of delirium, but his single-minded goal kept him going—he had to make it.

After a few minutes, his vision blurred, and he staggered like a drunk, his pace slowing dramatically. He didn't notice the two police officers rushing toward him, nor did he hear their commands: "Stop! Police! Stay where you are!"

He stumbled a few more steps before collapsing forward onto the ground.

The officers tried to rouse him, but when they couldn't, they called for an ambulance. While one officer administered first aid, performing chest compressions to keep Lennart alive, the other rummaged through his bag and pulled out his wallet. Taking Lennart's ID, he radioed in for a background check. "Requesting a check on Lennart Neumann, German national, ID number..." he relayed to the station.

Within a minute, they knew they had found Lennart, who had been reported missing nearly two weeks ago. Without pause, the officer performing first aid continued his efforts, rhythmically compressing Lennart's chest and checking if he was breathing.

Five minutes later, the paramedics arrived. The doctor immediately recognized Lennart's symptoms—his cramped hands and lips—and diagnosed hyperventilation. As they placed him on the stretcher, a paramedic held a rubber bag over Lennart's mouth, allowing him to breathe in his exhaled, oxygen-depleted air.

"He'll be fine. It's nothing serious—he's just hyperventilating," the doctor reassured.

Slowly, Lennart began to regain consciousness as the effects of the oxygen spray wore off. As he was loaded into the ambulance, one of the officers asked, "Can you hear me, Mr. Neumann? Can I ask you a few questions? Where have you been? You've been missing and listed in our system for days!"

Lennart, his muscles gradually relaxing, responded without hesitation, "I was on another world. I've finally made it back."

The officer nodded, his expression unreadable, and gave the ambulance driver a knowing glance. "Right... Good to have you back! The paramedics will take you to the hospital for a check-up. They'll help you if you need anything."

As the ambulance doors closed behind Lennart, the officer walked to the driver's side and spoke briefly to the paramedic. "Clearly a case for the psychiatric unit. I'll speak to the jogger and try to calm her down—maybe convince her not to press charges. After that, I'll head to the hospital to finish the paperwork. We can close the missing person case and notify his family."

The officer handed Lennart's bag to the paramedic, waved silently, and watched the ambulance drive off before turning back to the frightened jogger.

Not long after, Lennart was already feeling much better, but one pressing thought suddenly occupied his mind. On the way to the hospital, he remembered what Todax and Zafina had told him about what people would do if they found out where he had truly been. He needed a plausible explanation for his long absence.

A light bulb went on in his head. First, he needed to get changed quickly—anything to avoid ending up in a padded cell.

"Damn it! My bag with my clothes is gone," he exclaimed in shock.

The paramedic reassured him:

"Don't worry, Mr. Neumann. Your bag is in the driver's cabin. You'll get it back as soon as we arrive at the clinic."

But what could he possibly say? The truth would only bring him endless problems. So, by the time they reached the hospital, Lennart had pieced together an official story he could stick to. He knew he'd have to use it repeatedly. Lennart decided he would only tell the full truth to his parents and Felix. For the rest of the world, his carefully crafted explanation would be: "I had a car breakdown late at night after shopping near the woods. My phone was dead. With no help in sight, I walked through the forest towards my apartment. I got injured along the way. While seeking shelter, I accidentally fell into an old bunker. That made my injuries worse. I had to stay there until I recovered enough to free myself. During that time, I survived on the groceries I had bought. Once I got out, I was exposed to the elements, so I smeared wild berries I found on my skin to avoid getting sunburned in the heat. Eventually, I saw someone and screamed for help. They called the police, and now, finally, I've been rescued."

It wasn't a perfect story, Lennart thought, but it was the best he could come up with on short notice. At least the beginning was rooted in the truth.

By the time they reached the psychiatric hospital, Lennart was feeling much better. Despite being a bit drained after his ordeal, he was physically in great shape. He was back, and that filled him with immense joy.

The paramedic handed him his bag, and in the waiting room at the admissions station, Lennart quickly changed into fresh clothes. The doctors conducted a check-up but found no physical injuries. Nonetheless, they advised him to stay for one night under observation, just in case there were any signs of mental health issues.

Before being taken to his assigned room, Lennart requested permission to make two phone calls, as his phone was dead.

The first call he made, through tears, was to his parents. He gave them the address of the hospital and briefly explained what had happened. He didn't want to reveal the full truth over the phone, especially in the presence of medical staff, who might think he'd lost his mind.

After the emotional call with his parents, he dialed Felix's home number. Unfortunately, he didn't know Felix's mobile number by heart, only having it saved in his phone. When no one answered at Felix's house, Lennart decided he'd call back later, hoping to find a way to charge his phone.

He followed the nurse, who was taking him to his room for the night. As they walked down the hallway, the sound of his mother's tearful voice, filled with relief, and his father's calm, reassuring tone still echoed in his mind. His parents had promised to catch the next train and come to him immediately.

He could hardly wait. He had longed for this moment. He had hoped for it with all his heart.

13. Unexpected

Felix was sitting in his hospital room with his back to the door. Lunch had been served a few minutes earlier. The food wasn't particularly tasty, but it was better than struggling at home to cook himself something decent. The medication he was on made him indifferent to life in general. Nothing seemed to matter anymore.

He heard the knock on the door but didn't bother to turn around; he wasn't expecting his mother to visit at this time. Felix continued eating leisurely without even glancing over his shoulder.

The nurse swung the door open with a cheerful, "Hello there! I've brought you a new patient. He'll be staying just one night." Before she could say more, Lennart stepped in and asked her, "My phone's dead, and I really need to call my best friend Felix. Do you happen to have a charger here?"

The nurse shook her head but promised to check at the nurses' station before leaving the room.

Felix froze, his fork slipping from his hand. Slowly, he turned toward the new arrival. He had, of course, recognized Lennart's voice immediately. Looking at him as though he were seeing a ghost, Felix stared in disbelief, his eyes scanning Lennart from head to toe. Stuttering, he stood up and asked, "Lenni? You're alive? Thank God! What on earth happened to you? And why are you covered in paint?"

It hit Lennart like a bolt of lightning. Before he could say a word, he rushed to Felix, pulling him into a tight hug, refusing to let go. He whispered into Felix's ear, "Felix, as long as we're alone, I'll tell you everything. But be prepared—it's going to be hard to believe. Only you and my parents will know the truth. For everyone else, I've come up with a story. Earlier, when I was at the police station, I accidentally let a bit too much slip, and now I've ended up here. But first, you have to tell me why you're in the hospital!"

Felix's eyes widened in shock. He was desperate to understand what had happened to his best friend—what had made him disappear for so long.

Lennart began recounting his ordeal: the car breaking down late at night, getting injured in the forest, and limping around in search of shelter. He told Felix how he had fallen into a deep pit, breaking nearly every bone in his body, and how he had found himself, wracked with pain, in a secret Nazi bunker.

Felix listened intently, nodding occasionally but remaining silent. When Lennart described the infernal machine that had flung him into another world, Felix audibly gulped.

Lennart continued, undeterred, telling Felix how he was suddenly transported to a world where humans couldn't breathe. He explained how he and other beings were kept in habitats—how he met the transparent creature, the feathered ape-man, Todax, and the many other species. He spoke about Eugen, the formidable Abron, the just ruler Lemar, and his love for Zafina.

The more Lennart talked about his adventures, about his repeated escape attempts and failures, the more incredulous Felix's expression became. But Lennart pressed on, undeterred and animated. He explained how he had tried to disguise himself using the Ulam fruit and how its color stubbornly refused to come off. He described dying multiple times and being brought back to life, the alien world of Allcon with its moons, and every detail he could remember.

He ended his hour-long story with the moment he finally found freedom in the bunker and the terrified jogger who called the police.

Felix sat there, dumbfounded, struggling to process it all.

A Brief Pause

For a moment, there was silence. Then Felix cautiously interjected in a calm, soothing voice:

"Well, I can follow you up to the point where you fell into the Nazi bunker. But are you sure that everything after that wasn't just a hallucination? Maybe you hit your head during the fall and blacked out?"

Lennart responded, visibly agitated, "For God's sake, you don't believe me! Look at this!" He hastily showed Felix his pale lilac-colored hands and pulled a white garment out of his bag. "See this? This is what everyone on Allcon wears! This material isn't from Earth. Any lab would confirm that. These fibers and the way it's stitched don't exist here!"

Felix didn't want to hurt Lennart's feelings, but the story sounded like a fairy tale—so fantastical that he simply couldn't believe it. To avoid upsetting him further, Felix carefully steered the conversation in a different direction.

"Please forgive me, Lenni, if I seem a bit out of it. These meds they're giving me are pretty strong. But I want you to know, deep down, I'm so happy you're back."

He explained how much his life had changed since Lennart's disappearance. Shifting the topic not only helped him dodge Lennart's wild story but gave him a chance to share how things had gone downhill for him. In a trembling voice, Felix started with Nicole and Evelyn. He went on to describe the police raid and unexpected house search, his arrest, getting fired from his job, and eventually spiraling into a manic depression. He explained that he could no longer manage his life on his own and how Nicole had visited him here in the clinic but ultimately cut ties with him for good.

Lennart, deeply moved, lowered his head.

"Hey, I'm so incredibly sorry that my disappearance caused you so much pain. If I could undo it all, I would. The fact that you didn't give up on me means the world," Lennart said sincerely.

A knock at the door interrupted them, and the nurse who had accompanied Lennart earlier entered with a charging cable. She handed it to him with a polite request to return it to the nurses' station in two hours, then left.

As Lennart plugged in his phone, Felix suddenly jumped up.

"Speaking of phones, I need to call my parents and give them the good news!"

While dialing, Felix promised Lennart he wouldn't tell them about Allcon—they wouldn't believe it anyway. Lennart looked relieved.

When Felix's mother picked up, he exclaimed excitedly into the receiver, "Mom, Lenni's back! He just got admitted as my roommate. What a coincidence! He's fine, and I'm feeling amazing. So much so that I'm going to request discharge tomorrow!"

The call was brief, and fragments of the conversation floated through the air:

"...Yes, I'm sure! ...You're coming to visit later, right? Then he can tell you himself. ...Okay, see you soon!"

He hung up and passed on greetings from his parents to Lennart.

The two decided to step out into the hospital garden for some fresh air. As they walked, Lennart patiently answered all the questions Felix had been dying to ask. Just before they headed back to the room, Felix stopped and said:

"Lenni, my old friend, I don't mean to offend you, and you know you can trust me with anything. But I just can't wrap my head around you being stranded 40 light-years from Earth on a highly advanced world.

Maybe you were just knocked out after that brutal fall. The brain can play some cruel tricks on us."

Lennart wasn't angry, but it saddened him that his best friend didn't believe him.

"I guess I'll have to prove it to you. Not today, but soon. But please, let's stick to the official story for everyone else. Otherwise, I'll never get out of the psych ward," Lennart said, sounding slightly miffed.

He couldn't stop smiling.

He was overjoyed to be home again, with his best friend by his side. Being able to breathe normally and move freely once more felt like the greatest gift he could have received. When they returned to their room, dinner was being served. There was a vegetarian option and one with meat. Felix was astonished when Lennart chose the vegetarian dish—he had always been a passionate meat lover.

"I'm a vegetarian now," Lennart explained. "I feel sorry for the poor animals. I don't want to support this barbaric treatment of the beautiful creatures on our planet anymore."

Before he started eating, Lennart quickly returned the charging cable and, for the first time in ages, turned his phone on. For several minutes, the phone didn't stop buzzing—one notification after another flooded in: orders, emails, text messages. The constant beeping followed them through most of dinner.

"Wow, Felix, things are really happening online for me," Lennart said, barely intelligible with his mouth full. "And since you lost your job because of me, and I can't handle all these orders on my own, it would make sense for you to join me. I'd be thrilled if you did."

Felix immediately agreed to the idea; it was exactly what he needed. But the most touching moment was still to come. Without knocking, the door burst open, and Lennart's parents stormed into the room, tears streaming down their faces.

His mother cried out with joy and wrapped him tightly in her arms, sobbing louder and louder:

"I'll never let you go again, my boy!"

His father joined the embrace, hugging them both at once, unable to hold back his own tears. Slowly, they all calmed down. At first, Lennart's parents thought Felix was just visiting and were surprised to learn that he happened to be a patient in the same room.

They bombarded Lennart with questions: what had happened to him, and why had he ended up in a psychiatric clinic with purple skin? So Lennart told them everything from the beginning. Without a moment's hesitation, they believed his entire story and agreed, for his safety, to stick to the official "earthly" version for everyone else.

Felix also shared what had happened to him and how he had become a patient at the clinic. Lennart's mother then hugged Felix tightly as well, expressing her heartfelt sympathy and thanking him for doing everything in his power to search for Lennart. She condemned Felix's employer for their actions and lamented how people had treated him. Then she said, with a relieved heart:

"Who knows what good might come out of all this? But one thing I do know for sure—everything will be fine now!"

Everyone agreed. As Lennart answered all the lingering questions about his adventure, the atmosphere became more relaxed.

Lennart left it up to Felix to decide what version of events to share with his own parents. But Felix admitted:

"I know my parents—they're the kindest people on Earth. But even I'm struggling to follow this story. As much as they'd try to understand, they need a rational explanation."

Not long after, the room became even more crowded. Felix's parents walked in with open arms, and the welcome was as warm as it was emotional. With everyone together, Lennart's and Felix's parents used the joyful occasion to officially get to know one another—and they hit it off immediately. It was an unforgettable evening for everyone involved.

The next day, both Felix and Lennart voluntarily checked out of the clinic. For the first few days, they went their separate ways. Each had a lot to process and plenty to take care of. Felix stopped taking his prescribed medication entirely, with no adverse side effects.

Before long, they started meeting up frequently, just as they had planned, and began working together. Felix regularly delivered the 3D-printed items to the post office, while Lennart handled the writing and printing side of the business. Their arrangement worked remarkably well. At first, they divided the work so that Lennart could avoid going out too often. But after about two more weeks, Lennart's skin returned to its natural color.

Once things settled, they spent a lot of time together outside of work, talking often. These conversations helped both of them process everything that had happened. Surprisingly, since his return, Lennart had truly not eaten a single bite of meat—and Felix eventually followed his lead.

Lennart also developed a newfound peace with insects. While he still found mosquito bites unpleasant, he seemed to have come to terms with their existence. He never harmed a fly and treated every living creature with respect and love, believing each had its place in the world.

But there was one lingering issue between the two friends, a topic so heavy that neither dared to address it directly. The longer they avoided it, the more it seemed to grow into a silent rift.

Whenever Lennart talked about his experiences on Allcon—about Zafina or the Todax—Felix would listen patiently. But there was always a subtle shift in his expression, a barely noticeable twitch at the corners of his mouth.

To Lennart, it was clear: Felix didn't believe a word he said.

Finally, one evening after work, the tension boiled over, and the long-avoided conversation exploded into a confrontation.

14. Proof

After a productive day at work, Lennart suggested to Felix that they should wind down with a beer at a nearby beer garden. Felix agreed, and on that hot summer day, they drove there in Felix's car. The windows were rolled down, and the warm breeze blew against Lennart's face.

As they drove through a tree-lined avenue, Lennart casually said to Felix, "You know, I kind of feel sorry for that poor devil, Eugen. He spent his entire life in that habitat. It's such a blessing to be here with you, buddy, enjoying this freedom. That could have been me."

Lennart glanced over at Felix, who was focused on driving, and noticed with surprise that Felix was once again pulling that odd expression—his mouth subtly twisting. Lennart couldn't hold back and addressed him directly:

"Hey, man, you might not realize it, but I've noticed that every time I talk about my hellish experience, you make that same face. I can tell you still don't believe me. Should I have just told you half the truth?"

Felix replied almost reflexively, with a casual shrug:

"Come on, you've got to admit, it's hard to wrap my head around what you're saying. How would you react if I came back with a story like that, after everyone was sick with worry and nearly gave up hope of ever seeing you alive again?"

Lennart nodded sadly.

"Ah, so it's just a story to you? Do you have any idea how close I was to ending my own life, just to escape? And then waking up, realizing I had failed? It doesn't matter what you say now. You're coming with me into that damn bunker. You'll see for yourself that every word I told you is true. And after that, we're never having this conversation again."

When they arrived at the beer garden and got their drinks, the tension between them was palpable. Both sat in silence for a while. Finally, Lennart broke it:

"I really didn't want to see that nightmare of a bunker ever again. But for the sake of our friendship, I think I have to. Let's go there tomorrow. We'll take some gear to make sure things don't go south again."

Felix looked at him, surprised.

"What are you planning to do? How exactly are you going to prove this to me? Are you planning to beam me to some distant planet?" he asked, grinning ear to ear, clearly skeptical.

"No, not that. But there's something I promised the Allconians, something I need to finish," Lennart said seriously.

He flagged down a passing waiter and asked if he could borrow a notepad and pen. He began jotting down a list: long rope, hammer, screwdriver, long stick, flashlights, clothing, a bouquet of flowers, and phones. Confidently, Lennart tore the page off, handed the waiter's supplies back, and stuffed the list in his pocket.

He asked Felix to pick him up early the next morning, explaining that it might take a while to find the spot again. Though Felix still didn't fully believe him, a sense of unease crept over him. Cautiously, Felix said:

"Hey, you don't have to prove anything to me. Let's just drop it."

But his words had the opposite effect. Lennart shook his head.

"No, we're doing this. Once and for all. I've got everything we need. If you have an extra flashlight, bring it. And your phone—you always have that with you anyway."

The Next Morning

Bright and early, Felix arrived ten minutes ahead of schedule, but Lennart was already waiting outside his house. A fully packed backpack hung over his shoulder, with the handle of a large umbrella sticking out of it. The sight of Lennart, standing in the blazing sun under a perfectly clear blue sky, holding an umbrella, was almost comical.

In each hand, he held a cup of coffee. He handed one to Felix through the open driver's window and placed the other into the car's cupholder. Tossing his backpack onto the backseat, Lennart climbed into the car.

"Alright, Felix, buddy, let's hit the road," Lennart said, taking a small sip of his still-piping-hot coffee.

"Hey, thanks for the coffee, Lenni. I really needed this," Felix replied with a grin.

"Where are we going? I still have the location marked on the GPS where your car broke down," Felix asked groggily, still not fully awake. He took a sip from his steaming cup.

Lennart replied, "No, that's way too far from the bunker. Better we head to where the police picked me up."

They set off, with Lennart guiding Felix to the small forest road where he had chased the frightened jogger. They parked the car on the unpaved roadside and started walking toward the forest. For a good half hour, they trekked deeper into the dense woods, with Lennart scanning the surroundings intently.

"It should be around here somewhere!" he muttered to Felix, explaining the marker he had left: a stack of stones a few steps away from the overgrown ventilation shaft. Despite both of them searching for the marker, it initially seemed futile.

Then Felix noticed what looked like the stack on a small hill and pointed it out to Lennart with an outstretched finger. Lennart's heart raced instantly. "Bullseye, Felix! That's it!" he exclaimed, rushing to the overgrown spot he had further concealed with leaves when he left. Quickly, he began removing the camouflage.

"Okay, Felix. We'll need to lower the rope here. Let's tie it to that tree over there," Lennart instructed, pulling a long coiled rope from his backpack. They secured it tightly with a double knot and dropped it into the dark, eerie depths below.

Lennart threw his bag through the opening, letting it fall. Then, he squeezed through himself and slid down the rope.

"Your turn!" came his muffled voice from the dark below.

Felix suddenly felt uneasy. Fear crept in. At first, he hadn't believed Lennart, but now his story was starting to feel all too real. Without a word, Felix followed and lowered himself into the bunker.

Lennart switched on his flashlight.

"Did you bring yours? The more light, the better," he asked confidently.

Felix nodded and pulled a small but bright LED flashlight from his pocket, his hand trembling. He looked around the room, overwhelmed by what he saw. This was far from what he had expected.

"Wait a moment, buddy. I want to see if the iron bar I used to smash the equipment left any damage," Lennart said as he flipped the main switch with both hands.

Suddenly, the room lit up. The machines buzzed, creaked, and roared back to life. Both men jumped back in shock.

"Damn it! It's not broken! But I smashed every console I could reach with that bar!" Lennart whispered to Felix, his voice quivering.

Summoning his courage, Lennart retrieved a ceremonial Allconer robe and a small bouquet of roses still wrapped in plastic from his bag. He spread the robe across the bed-like platform in the center of the room and placed the flowers on top. Then, he removed the key around his neck—the symbol of his escape—and laid it alongside them.

Next, Lennart pulled out the large umbrella from his bag. Using its handle to keep a safe distance, he flipped the activation lever on the armrest and quickly retreated to Felix. The machines grew louder, forcing Lennart to raise his voice so Felix could hear.

"Now watch what happens to those items!" Lennart shouted over the din.

A vortex of increasingly dense light enveloped the platform until a loud bang silenced the machinery, plunging the room into darkness.

Both men stared at the platform, dumbfounded. The flowers and robe were gone.

"See? I was lying on that bed, gravely injured after the fall, and this machine catapulted me to another world. Now you have to believe me!" Lennart said, slightly offended.

Felix stood there, mouth agape and eyes wide. After a few seconds, he managed to speak, placing a trembling hand on Lennart's shoulder.

"Holy… You poor guy! I'll never doubt your story again. Please forgive me for not believing you at first. But let's get out of here—I can't stay here a second longer."

Lennart nodded.

"Gladly, but I made a promise to the Allconers," he said, pulling a heavy hammer and screwdriver from his backpack.

He handed Felix the screwdriver and tasked him with unscrewing a warning sign that read "Danger: High Voltage" from the wall as a memento, while Lennart set about smashing the machinery.

This time, parts of the machine came flying off as Lennart swung the hammer wildly. He didn't stop until he was utterly exhausted. To ensure his job was complete, he tested the main switch one last time. Nothing happened.

He had kept his word to Todax and Zafina.

After climbing out of the bunker using the stacked stones and rope, both men felt a wave of relief. Before heading back to the car, Lennart covered the ventilation shaft with plants and leaves so thoroughly that no one would ever find the bunker again. This time, he left no marker. He had no intention of ever returning.

The only thing Lennart kept to remember this adventure was the warning sign, a tribute to the extraordinary beings who had taught him so much about grace and true love—lessons he hadn't understood at first but had come to value deeply.

Even Felix changed after that day in the Nazi bunker. He realized he should not be so quick to dismiss things, no matter how improbable they might seem. He now believed the universe teemed with life.

Of course, life eventually returned to normal for both of them. Months later, the events felt like a distant, blurry dream to Lennart. Yet, when he was alone, he often thought back to his time on Allcon with great fondness, vividly recalling Zafina's beautiful eyes. In those moments, he silently whispered to her, "I love you."

Acknowledgments

Luis Feder: Author

I would like to express my heartfelt gratitude to:

Phill – You are not only my son but the very purpose of my life. I am so proud of you, my big little one.

Mom – I hope you know this: Without you, I'd be nothing.

You both believed in me and saw potential in me. A huge THANK YOU for that!

My gratitude also extends to many others who helped and supported me. I hope none of you feel slighted if your names are not explicitly mentioned—there are simply too many to list. You know who you are.

Above all, my thanks go to you, dear readers. Thank you for immersing yourselves in my world of thoughts and embarking on this mental journey to a far-off place with me.

Special thanks:

- OpenAI with ChatGPT: For translations from German.